ORCA
YOUNG
READERS

D0384165

Under a
Living Sky

Joseph Simons

ORCA BOOK PUBLISHERS

National Library of Canada Cataloguing in Publication Data
Simons, Joseph, 1956-
Under a living sky / Joseph Simons.

(Orca young readers)
ISBN 1-55143-355-9

1. Depressions—1929—Saskatchewan—Juvenile fiction.
I. Title. II. Series.

PS8637.I48U54 2005   jC813'.6   C2005-904616-3

First published in the United States, 2005
Library of Congress Control Number: 2005930967

Summary: At the height of the Depression, Mary is unlikely to receive
new shoes for Christmas but is deeply disappointed to receive a doll
crudely sewn from a horse's nosebag instead.

Free teachers' guide available at www.orcabook.com

Orca Book Publishers gratefully acknowledges the support for its
publishing programs provided by the following agencies: the Government of
Canada through the Department of Canadian Heritage's Book Publishing
Industry Development Program (BPIDP), the Canada Council for the Arts,
and the British Columbia Arts Council.

Cover design and typesetting by Lynn O'Rourke
Cover & interior illustrations by John Beder

In Canada:
Orca Book Publishers
PO Box 5626, Stn. B
Victoria, BC Canada
V8R 6S4

In the United States:
Orca Book Publishers
PO Box 468
Custer, WA USA
98240-0468

www.orcabook.com
Printed and bound in Canada
08 07 06 05 • 6 5 4 3 2 1

In memory of John Doerksen,
who told me this story,
and with gratitude to his daughter,
Karen, who helped me to write it.

Chapter 1

The little spot, perfectly round and clear, had begun to frost over. Mary pressed her nose against the window to make another. She was carrying out an experiment. How much heat would it take to make a small clearing in the sheet of ice that lined the big parlor window? Her nose felt quite cold already. It took a lot of heat, she decided, just to make one little clear spot. And when it was made, you couldn't see much through so small a clearing.

The ice had stopped in mid-ooze, like a crowd of white paint people caught running and commanded to sit still, by golly, unless they wanted a chore or two to steady them down.

A muffled call came from above, Mother's. Mary cocked her head, which was difficult because her nose had to be kept tight to the pane of glass. Meanwhile the window breathed in and out, shrieking at the seams and flexing forcefully because of the wind outside. Mary did not reply, and in answer to her non-reply she could feel Mother's aggravation growing. Impatient footsteps sounded on the floorboards of the room above her.

"Mary Elizabeth Vannieuwenhuizen! Do you hear me? You get up here this minute! If you don't clean up your room, Christmas won't come, or not for you anyway!"

Mary sighed. She didn't know why Mother was angry this time. As Papa often said, bedrooms were only a place to sleep. He also said it was a full-time job these days to guess what would set Mother off. Mary wished Mother would stop being upset and give her some peace for a change. All at once, making little round clearings in that big sighing window seemed a lot less fun. Mary slumped down onto the sofa. Feeling her nose, so numb with cold, she smiled. She gave herself both an "A" and a gold star for her experiment.

There was a crack in the side of her shoe. Wiggling her big toe, Mary stretched open the crack, easier to open every week. Not that the shoe was hers, she thought. This shoe was Judith's, an annoying shoe, an annoying sister's annoying shoe. These shoes of Judith's had been passed down to Mary last spring. No, no, no, said Mary to herself, my shoes will be brand new, not worn out by Judith, not worn ever by anybody. They will not be cracked and scuffed. She sighed. It was pleasant to sit on the sofa and dream of shoes never worn by a soul. They were sure to arrive any day now, maybe the very next day.

"Mary Elizabeth!" Another familiar voice, Judith's, piped down the stairs. The notes wavered but ended just like Mother's. No, more shrilly, more like the squeak of a prairie dog caught by a hawk. Mary rolled her eyes at the ceiling. Judith had to repeat every command. She seemed to know what Mother wanted more often than not.

Since her eyes were on the ceiling anyway, Mary studied the angel, the yellow places where rain had leaked in and spread during a fall storm. Papa, although happy to get some rain, had had to go on the roof to put hot tar on the leaky spots. Mary liked seeing the angel up there, arms open wide, ready to laugh and play, never shrill.

Then two things happened at once. Mother's voice went as shrill as Judith's, reaching a point that might be called spanking mad. And the back door opened. It opened with a welcome bang that interrupted the repeated callings of her name. Mary ran gratefully from the warm front room to a kitchen already filled with cold air. A snowstorm was blowing in there. Papa was pulling in the tree. Its green branches bounced over the floor.

Following Papa was her little brother, Joseph. Bound by layers of clothing, Joseph waddled like a penguin and spun on the wet floor. Mary ran to help him shut the door. They pushed and pushed, but the door would not close. The floor was slippery with snow, and the wind was firm as a rock. Papa laughed. "You two make quite a team," he said. He gave the door a thump with a big mitted hand. The wind ceased instantly, and the kitchen became silent, except in the stove, where knots of burning wood exploded with regular bangs and whistled up the pipe.

On the floor lay a tree, a bright green tree, strangely out of place inside a house.

"Mary Elizabeth." Mother spoke from the bottom of the stairs. Her voice was deadly quiet now, the way it got when she was so angry that every word had to be measured. Even Papa looked up at the tone, and Mary watched him instead of turning to Mother. "You get up there this instant and help your sister like I said."

Mary glanced over. Judith was there too, but higher up, peering triumphantly around the corner of the landing. Her straight brown hair lay draped like old weeds over the railing.

"A messy room won't matter for an hour," said Papa gruffly. He was taking off his coat, big and sheepskin soft, with its tattered wool cuffs. "Or a day neither, come to think of it." His coat hung on the wooden peg by the door, Papa bent to unwind Joseph, who stood nearby, mute and puffed into a state of immobility inside hat, scarves, mittens and coats.

The furrow on Mother's forehead told Mary that she was

not out of the woods yet. Mary peeked up at Judith. Her sister's narrowing eyes let Mary know that some little thing would happen later to make up for this tiny victory over Mother, and so over herself. Judith would, as usual, even the score after bedtime.

Joseph was peeled out of his outer clothes by Mother, who had brushed Papa away. Stronger than words, her quick actions told everyone that he was incompetent with children, even down to simple chores like dressing them. Papa frowned a moment, but then saw Mary. He must have noticed how she was getting sad, she thought, for he winked and said, "Come on, Mary. Let's get this tree up."

Mary held one of the icy branches with its sharp needles while he carried most of the tree into the living room. They inserted the trunk into the red-painted tree holder already in the corner. The tree looked very nice standing by itself. Its green needles were bright against the blanket that Mother had hung to curtain off the leaky window and the front door. This door wasn't used all winter because she'd stuffed the cracks around it with cardboard to keep out the draft.

"Lovely," said Papa. "Don't you think, Ruthie?"

"Very fetching."

In the doorway, Mother stood with her arms crossed. Joseph's plump arm circled one of her thighs. Judith poked her head past them, sawing her skinny neck against the

doorjamb. Mary looked up to the angel in the ceiling and wished that Christmas day would somehow be happier than these last months. Angels were supposed to bring good news, weren't they? Happy news? I'd even give up my new shoes for some peace and quiet, she told the angel. Studying her old shoes, she added, But only if there's no other way.

Chapter 2

Mary hardly slept all night for thinking about the new unused shoes. They'd be her Christmas present. They just had to be. As she lay awake in the bed with Judith, she reviewed the promise Mother had made in the fall, when Mary's toes had been pushing out the front of her old shoes, which were really Judith's old shoes. "You'll have to wear these of Judith's for a while," Mother had said as her fingers laced the shoes roughly to Mary's feet.

"But Mother, they flop on me like ducks' feet."

"Well, if Saint Nicholas and Black Peter don't leave a lump of coal in your sock, maybe they'll bring you new shoes. Or maybe next fall, if you start school, and if we can afford them."

Mary always remembered the rare smile and the moment of tenderness. It seemed impossible that her year's worth of deeds would get her only a lump of coal. Generally the

Saint Nicholas and Black Peter story seemed designed to keep children in their place, but since that moment, Mary was convinced that Mother really did mean to get her shoes this Christmas. Nobody in living memory ever got a lump of coal. She fell asleep with happy thoughts of new shoes, of wearing shoes that fit, of school next fall.

In the morning, a sharp pain in her hip told Mary it must be time to get up. She wished Judith wouldn't be so fast to pinch her in the morning. After all, there was no fun in getting up in a cold room. Judith had dressed already. She flaked the covers on and off Mary. It was futile to say or do anything. Judith was much stronger and seemed able to fashion new torments as she needed them. And whatever Mary said or did always made things worse.

When Judith grew bored of tormenting her sister, she left the room. Mary took a deep breath, slipped off her flannel nightie and sprang into her cold clothes. Oh, they were cold! She ran by Joseph's bed, a small nest low in the corner, empty. She ran down the stairs, cold but happy. Christmas had come at last.

Downstairs, Joseph played on the floor with lettered building blocks and an old toy wagon. The blanket was drawn back from the window, and Judith was staring out its only tiny clear corner. Mary hopped on the sofa too. Using her breath to soften the ice, she scraped a clearing of her own. The ice was softer today than last night, easier to scrape. Using the building block with the letter "S" on it—"S" for shoes—she cleared enough window to see that new snow had fallen. A light frosting of white covered the old snow. The snowman wore a clean white toque set so stylishly it reminded Mary of a dashing young man in the Eaton's cataloge. The wind had died down in the night.

It began to snow again, a snowfall so heavy the granary disappeared. The corner of the barn, usually visible from the parlor window, went with it. Snow had filled in every crack and footprint. Papa's path to the barn, a hard channel cut into deep snow by use, was now a gently snaking valley, a miniature of the big valley they lived in. And looking at her valley was Mary's first and most necessary duty every morning. But this morning there was hardly a trace of the valley to look at. The usual wispiness of the dawn, the streaks of snow blowing across frozen fields, in fact everything past the snowman was hidden in the heavy snowfall. It was like being alone in a sudden fog. But the long wide valley was out there, Mary knew, and this valley was hers.

"Strange to go to church on a Friday," said Judith, flopping down. She twisted her body and looked at the tree, festively decorated with popcorn and colored-paper angels and antelope. The scent of spruce pitch filled the room. Only the treetop star was missing. "But maybe we won't go to church at all."

Mary eyed Judith warily. Was this plain statement to be

taken as a moment of honesty or was it a trick to get her into trouble? Judith stared at the tree, smiling innocently. Today being Christmas, Mary decided she'd risk agreeing with Judith. "I hope we can stay home too."

She turned to watch out the window for Papa. Presently he emerged from the curtain of white flakes. Another gust came, and the flakes swirled upward so that the end of his scarf played up behind him like a dog's tail. He stepped high, following the blown-in path, and butterflies of white snow swarmed around him. He carried a milk pail, which steamed and scraped across the low-crested drifts.

Mary ran back into the kitchen. Mother's hips moved gently as she stirred milk and eggs into a bowl. Eyes half-closed, she stood at the counter in front of the tiny window. Mother couldn't have seen much because that window was frosted over too. Mary was ready for Papa when he walked through the kitchen door. Before he could even set down the milk pail, and hardly before he could get the door closed, she hugged him at his hips and shouted, "Merry Christmas, Papa!"

He reached down to her. The pail clunked on the floor. He picked her up. The metal handle clinked as it fell against the milk pail's side. He put his cold bristly face against her warm one and said, "Merry Christmas, sweetheart."

The flapjacks hissed as the batter dropped spoon by spoon into the big black frying pan. Mary felt sorry for not saying something nice to Mother. So she wiggled down out of Papa's arms and ran to Mother. "Merry Christmas, Mother!" she shouted.

Joseph came in wailing, his wooden wagon in one hand and a large black wheel in the other. He stopped, looked at Mary with large wondering eyes and began to jump up and down instead. He ran to them shouting as loudly as he could, confident that today he would get away with as much noise as he cared to make.

Then Judith came charging in, and the three of them clung to and leaped about Mother, shouting, "Merry Christmas, Mother!" She gave each child a hug, although quick and too businesslike for a real Christmas hug, and returned to spooning batter into the pan. But they wouldn't go away.

Setting the spoon on the stove, Mother reached down to give each of them another hug, each slightly longer than necessary. Then she said, "Come now. We have to get ready."

Papa was hanging up his coat. "Get ready for what?"

Mother's shoulders straightened. There was trouble coming.

"You're not actually wanting to go out, are you?"

"It's Christmas."

"Have you looked outside, Ruthie? No one will be there today. Or not if they have any sense, they won't."

Mother's brave smile turned to frost. With suddenly firm hands, she ushered the children to the table. One by one they were deposited roughly on their chairs.

Papa took his chair grimly. Mary felt afraid. Christmas was going to be like any other day. "It's storming out there, you know," said Papa. "Why put the children and yourself in danger?"

In answer, Mother dropped the tea basket into the little brown pot. This alone showed how special today was to her, and that Papa had better watch out. Because of their finances, Mother now brewed tea only on special days and Sundays, even though Papa grumbled about doing without. She clunked the teapot onto the table. There was a kind of finality about her way of slipping the bright blue cozy over the pot. There was no going back. Taking the mugs and plates from where they were warming on the stove, she set them on the table. Mary felt the crockery to see which parts were the warmest. She expected to burn her hand, probably need a trip in to the doctor. Her plate was not hot enough.

Yet empty warm plates in winter were sort of funny to think about, since plates were not alive like cows and chickens. This is a question I'll certainly ask next fall in school, Mary told herself. She was sure she'd be allowed to go this coming year, as the doctor had promised that the hole in her heart would heal by the time she was eight or nine.

Meanwhile, she'd missed a lot of school and resented it. How would she ever catch up? But Papa was afraid to let her go, afraid something bad would happen, something unforeseen. For two years, Mary had entertained herself with scenes of fainting spells in the schoolyard. Carried to a place of refuge, she'd wake up in a sunny room with frills on the bed and cakes on the side table. She felt her plate again. Why did animals and people have warmth in themselves, but things like plates and beds need to be warmed? In school she'd ask about filling the holes in people's hearts and many other smart questions. The teacher would adore her.

Her plate was no longer hot, nor was it empty. Two flap-jacks lay on it. Papa put a big yellow gob of butter on top. Giving her a wink, he poured her some milk from the clay jug. The fresh milk was skinned with warm foam. Mary buried her lip into the foam as Papa poured Joseph's milk. Judith poured her own after Papa handed her the jug.

Finally Mother sat down. They had all been waiting for her, not daring to touch their food. The butter was melting nicely. "Judith?" Mother said.

Judith bowed her head. "God is great. God is good," she chanted. Mary snuck a quick look. Judith had her eyes open. Her hard black pupils were directed unblinkingly at the pancakes losing steam on her plate. Papa did not bow his head. As if he had a backache, he studied the ceiling till grace was over.

"Let us thank him for our food," Judith finished.

"Ah-men," Mother said. Mary and Joseph and Judith all said the same, repeating "Ah-men" after Mother in the same solemn way. A strong blast of wind shook the kitchen, rattling the windowpane in its frame. The wind whistled in the stovepipe. The walls vibrated around them as if the house were flying through the air. They could hear the screech of the weather vane as it swung to meet the wind.

"They're singing now," said Papa, tearing his eyes from the stained ceiling. "Wind's turned." He poured the tea into the mugs and rested his gaze on Mary.

Mary's toes were cold. A draft went right through her sweater too. She thought of the stable and the angels, and shepherds bowing before heavenly messengers. "I hear them," she whispered. "I do."

"Who?" Joseph asked.

"Mother," said Judith, sounding offended. "Just this morning Mary was saying she didn't want to go to church."

Mary started at the sound of her name. There was the familiar triumph in Judith's pinched face. Mary looked down at her plate. She wanted to eat now. She didn't want to see the disapproval on Mother's face, nor the approval on Papa's. She didn't want either of them to ask why she would or would not want to stay home. Why did Judith

15

have to be so mean? Couldn't she be nice for a few minutes on Christmas morning?

"Who?" Joseph repeated, mouth full. Somehow a smear of butter had reached his forehead, slicking both eyebrows upward. He looked surprised by everything.

"Don't speak with your mouth full," Judith said. Prim as could be, she cut a small piece of pancake and bit it gently.

Papa looked at Judith with the blankest of expressions. The calf, whenever Mary offered him hay, always looked at her like this. She knew this was because calves ate only milk. Mary felt afraid. Papa sighed.

Suddenly the tension annoyed Mary even more than Judith and all her finking did. "I'll want to go if you want me to, Mother," she said.

"What I want isn't important, obviously." Picking up her mug of tea with both hands, Mother took a slow sip and then turned her gray eyes to Papa. "It's Christmas, and the children need to go. We all do."

"In a near blizzard." He stated it flatly, again like a calf.

"In a near blizzard," she answered, just as flatly. "If need be."

"I have to go," said Judith. "I'm in the play." Her eyes rolled back and forth over her milk glass, as if measuring the distance between her mother and her father.

16

Mary thought of the peacefulness of them all snuggled warmly under the quilts in the sleigh. It would be better than this. "Let's go, Papa," she urged.

Joseph was standing on his chair. His hands were planted flat on the table, and he still looked surprised as he leaned over his plate and shrieked, "WHO!?"

Chapter 3

"Whoa, Clyde," Papa said, pulling on the reins. Clyde and his cutter-load of people came to a sliding stop before the fence surrounding the playground. Papa threw back the quilts and hopped out. Cold air rushed over Mary's legs. Joseph wiggled with excitement beside her. Papa walked forward, patting Clyde's withers as he went along the shaft.

"Lots of people here, I see," Mother said.

Papa looked back, and so did Clyde, his breath streaming out in two long funnels. He was breathing fire. He was a dragon on the prowl, searching the street for tasty children, and there were a few. Papa just shook his head.

But it was true. Many children with their parents were coming together at the little schoolhouse, a building located on the edge of town. Some were parking horses and sleds in the drive-in shed of the church next door. Some were walking up the street from the heart of Davidson. Across

18

the road a man was blowing on his fingers and putting his head under the upright hood of his car. Two walkers bent forward into gusts of wind rushing around the grain elevator, which was a tall ghostly gray rising into the snow-swirled heavens. Scarves and arms flapped in the wind. Mary wondered if everyone would find a place to sit. The schoolhouse contained only a single large room.

Giving Clyde's head a scratch, Papa tied the lead rope to a post. Only then did he call back "Okay!" He returned and pulled a canvas nosebag of oats and a dirty blanket out from under the seat of the cutter. The blanket he threw over the horse's wet gray back.

Papa took a long slow look at the nosebag, fingering its old canvas thoughtfully before passing its strap over the big horse's high ears. The bag smothered the cones of steam puffing from Clyde's nostrils. The dragon became a plain old workhorse again, hitched to an old sled and wearing an old blanket that sailed off in the wind. Papa caught the blanket and wedged it between the shafts and Clyde's flanks. He knotted its corners into the harness.

Meanwhile Mother, on the other side of Judith, slid out and hurried her children from the cutter. They had to step carefully because the drift was high, well over the children's knees. "Watch out for each other," she said. "And stay clear of the traffic." Horses and sleighs trampled and swished past them all around the snow-swept yard.

"Hello, Ray!" shouted a man just driving by. He turned his horse and cutter into the deep drift before the next parking post. "How's my old gelding doing? Still pulling?"

"Pulling good, George!"

As Papa and George began a conversation over Clyde's broad rump, exposed and steaming due to the horse-blanket being too small, Mother pulled the children away. Mary heard no more of what they said. "We have to hurry to get a seat," Mother said.

Though she was nervous about all the people, Mary felt eager to meet them and jealous too. Judith was allowed to come here for school while she had to wait practically another year. She had often complained about the unfairness of it. "A whole 'nother year," Mary said, looking at the schoolhouse longingly. She hadn't been inside the place since last summer, when Papa had shown her the desk and bench where he'd sat as a boy.

"Talking to yourself now too?" Judith said.

Mary smelt wood smoke then, a brief whiff swallowed by the wind. The chimney was a rusty pipe shoved up into a white sky. But she could see no smoke. That tireless wind rushed everything away into the fluid and stormy morning.

"Must you dawdle, Mary? Come along." Mother pulled Mary's mitted hand sharply, then dropped it and stooped to pick up Joseph. "You two girls hold hands," she said over her shoulder. "And don't dawdle."

Judith held Mary's hand and dragged her along until Mother's back was turned. Then she pushed Mary off into a drift beside the path. Mary stepped onto the path again to follow at her own pace. She felt a spot of cold where snow entered her shoe through the big crack. Rather, it entered Judith's shoe. Near the entrance, Mary joined the line to mount the steps.

Judith was whining to Mother, "But she wouldn't keep up."

Not for the first time, Mary wished she had no sister. Everything would be easier without Judith. Don't cry now, she told herself, feeling her eyes prickle. Not on Christmas morning, and not in front of Judith. She looked away, wiped a disobedient tear from her eye and thought instead about her new shoes. They'd be waiting under the tree at home. Brand-new shoes of her very own.

They went into the schoolhouse and sat through the Christmas program. A confusing sea of big heads and red ears and wide hats with feathers turned with every action as students became biblical characters or helped with props. Two children holding up a curtain edged sideways to reveal an angel that Mary did not know. The angel told the Virgin that she would have a baby. The angel seemed nice. Mary expected that by this time next year, she and the angel would be friends. When asked about a room for the night, a ten-year-old innkeeper opened his mouth eagerly, croaked and shook his head without saying a word. The manger was filled with real hay but surrounded by strange-looking beasts like a cow that coughed, a sheep that hiccuped and a big-eared donkey that forgot itself completely and barked. There was no sign of Judith anywhere. Mary guessed the play must be going all wrong.

A rag-doll Jesus was produced, visited by jostling shepherds and sparkle-winged angels and turbaned wise men. The story took them from Bethlehem to Egypt, and on to Nazareth. The actors seemed lost. They milled about on stage and then stopped to stare down at something. No, someone.

As if commanded by the staring actors, the minister rose to his feet. He was laughing and applauding. Everyone clapped, and he led them in a Christmas carol. All the people sang, "Silent night, holy night, all is calm…" Mary sang too. The words floated upward with great feeling and got caught in the rafters, where before there was only the constant shriek of wind.

The minister prayed aloud, asking "blessings for every soul present" and closing, as he said, "quite a busy hour."

They filed outside, where Papa was waiting on the porch. "That storm's getting worse, Ruth. Look, the cathedral's all gone now." His thick arm pointed to where the grain elevator should have stood. The same arm swooped down to pick up Mary. Groaning over houses and horses and cars and people, the wind stretched along the wide street to its unseen end.

How did snow and wind make a tall elevator vanish? Another good question for the teacher. Under her breath, Mary began to sing, "Silent night, holy night, all is calm..."

"Aren't we going to the angle cans, Papa?" Joseph asked. His short arms were clasped around Mother's neck.

"Who?"

"Reverend Bartle said they were having a special communion service," explained Mother. "The Anglicans are inviting everyone to come and join them, and then there's a potluck lunch and games back here at the schoolhouse."

"And you want to go," mumbled Papa. He blinked uneasily up at the flakes of snow tumbling everywhere overhead. Nothing at all was visible beyond the tethered horses. "We get stuck here, Ruthie, there sure won't be no room at the inn."

Mother looked up at the peak of the schoolhouse. Snow was driving off it beautifully. "No, better not, I guess."

Mother glanced down at Judith. She looked very small with her head so far below them all. "You couldn't have spared a minute to come in and watch Judith do her part?" Mother asked. She turned to lead the way down the path.

"I was there, standing at the back, wasn't I, Judith?"

Judith was being herded forward between her two parents. "I didn't see you," she said sullenly.

23

Papa smiled into Mary's face and said, "Well, I suppose sheep are built to stare at the floor. That'll be why you didn't see me. But I was standing there, thinking, By gosh and by golly, she is a sheep, without a doubt."

"A sheep with hiccups!" Mary said, laughing as she realized where Judith had disappeared to during the play.

"Is it that you're ashamed to sit with us, then?" Mother threw her words forward, out into a little squall of flakes funneling up before her.

Mary looked at Papa. Was he ashamed of them?

He smiled. He wasn't going to be angry. He gave Mary a squeeze. "Just catching up on the gossip is all, Ruthie."

They arrived at the cutter. "What gossip?"

"Johnson says there's gonna be a war."

"He wants a war just to market his grain."

"I guess he hears it all on the radio."

Papa swept the snow from the single cold bench, and Mother tucked the children in. Clyde looked miserable. A snowdrift lay on his back, and icicles hung from his mane. His chin was thrown out bleakly. But at least the bag was off his face. He breathed large dragon breaths again.

Papa untied Clyde's blanket and lead line and backed him out of the row of sleighs. The snow squeaked under Clyde's hooves and under the cutter's runners too. Horses up and down the line, envious of the chance to move and yearning for their own warm barns, turned milky brown eyes toward them. A man two horses down waved. "Are you sure?"

Papa shouted back, "Can't afford it is all!"

"The Depression is over! The paper says so!"

"Oh, I don't believe that, and now we'll be into another goldarn war!"

"Raynold, don't swear, please." Mother settled on the bench.

"That's hardly swearing, Ruth."

"Maybe not, but you must mean it for swearing or you wouldn't do it."

Smiling guiltily, he swung into the sleigh.

"What's a war, Papa?" Mary knew what a war was, but it being Christmas, she hoped Papa would talk about a distant war rather than start a small one here and now with Mother.

He pulled the quilts around them both. "It's a time when men with money get men with no money to kill each other off. Home, Clyde. Giddy-up." Clyde only nodded and gave a small tug. "It ain't a request!" Flicking the reins, Papa slapped Clyde's wide icy rump. Clyde sighed and put his shoulder into the harness. They slid smoothly down the road that led out of town.

Chapter 4

"What can't we afford?" Mary asked. She hoped desperately Papa wouldn't say "shoes."

"A radio."

"Oh. That's good." It was nothing important.

They were shut in by snow. "Hope Clyde has his directions straight today," said Papa with a chuckle. He no longer seemed worried about the storm. "Well, we'll just follow along the wire for a bit anyway." The whipping gray telegraph wire hummed and sawed up in the snowy whiteness of the air to their right. "Sounds like an airyplane, don't it?"

"Don't know what an airyplane sounds like," said Mary. Only then did she notice Mother's silence, that solid wordless presence she'd kept since leaving town. This silence was not right for Christmas day. Mother could do what she liked on other days, but not today. "Do you, Mother?"

"No."

"You heard one at the fair," Judith said.

"I don't remember any airyplane."

After a few minutes of Clyde's slow and steady trotting, Judith said, "Why do we always have to be the first to leave?"

"Will you go?" Mother asked.

Nobody spoke. Everyone knew this question was directed at Papa. He drove with his blue eyes straight ahead for a while, then said, "I can't say. Have to see if we can get up a decent crop this year. If we can't, maybe we'll go where all the other neighbors go, if there's any room left, which would come as a surprise. Them other places must be full up by now."

"I don't want you to go," said Mother. "Or us to go."

"Army pays hard currency, at least. I don't know, Ruthie. I hope not."

Clyde snorted and tossed his head and swished his tail in front of them. His harness creaked as he paced on into the swirling snow and biting wind.

"And you really were standing in the back, back there?"

"On my toes in the clean air at the back," Papa answered. He reached his mitted hand and massive arm across the children's faces and patted Mother on her knee. He left his hand there a moment too. Mary saw it all.

She was thrilled. She glanced at Judith, who was smiling

too. Not wanting to catch her sister in a moment of weakness, Mary turned back to Clyde.

His tail swished back and forth among the snowflakes. Flecks of foam gathered at the seam where his rear legs joined his body. His horsey smell swept past them. Today Clyde did not clop. He thudded, for the snow was thick, even on this raised road. He went along steadily until they reached their track, where he turned off without being signalled.

"Wants his oats," said Papa. The wire thrummed wildly as they slid underneath it. "Here's one old boy that will move mountains for oats, make no mistake. And this time he may have to move mountains." Papa raised his arm and pointed ahead. Large drifts lay across the track, like winter's white arms stubbornly crossed. Ridge upon ridge of snow rumpled the treeless landscape ahead. A blast of wind, racing over these ridges, put the finishing touches on filling in the tracks they'd made only a couple of hours before.

Clyde plunged into the first drift. He dragged the cutter through. The second drift went well too, but more slowly. The third went more slowly yet. These were deep drifts. Finally Papa said, "Help's a-coming, Clyde, my boy." He jumped out and began to lift and push. Mother stepped out to help too, and he said, "That's all right, Ruthie. You can get back in."

"His legs are shaking." Mother went behind to push.

Papa handed the reins to Mary, who was closest, and Judith shot her a look of such meanness that Mary tried to give them back.

"No. It's easy," Papa assured her. "Just slow him down for me on the other side."

Then they were through. "Whoa," Mary said.

"Whoa, boy!" called Papa. "WHOA!"

Clyde was breathing hard and pulling hard on the reins. "Papa," said Mary, "I think he wants to try the next drift."

Judith snorted. So did Clyde.

Papa grabbed the reins. Pulling the horse to a stop, he said, "Maybe so. But maybe Clyde just wants to get home to his oats, and that drift happens to be in his way."

"He wants to get warm," Joseph said, his voice muffled by layers of clothing. He himself could not possibly be cold.

"See all that sweat," said Judith. "Anybody could see he's warm already."

"I'm sure he has a horsey reason," said Mother, breathing hard, "to get home."

Papa and Mother stood on the running boards for the shallow icy stretches, where the hard snow had been swept clean by the wind and could take the weight of the cutter. They jumped off to push in the softer drifts, where the slender runners sank in. Except for "Whoa!" and "Giddy-up!"

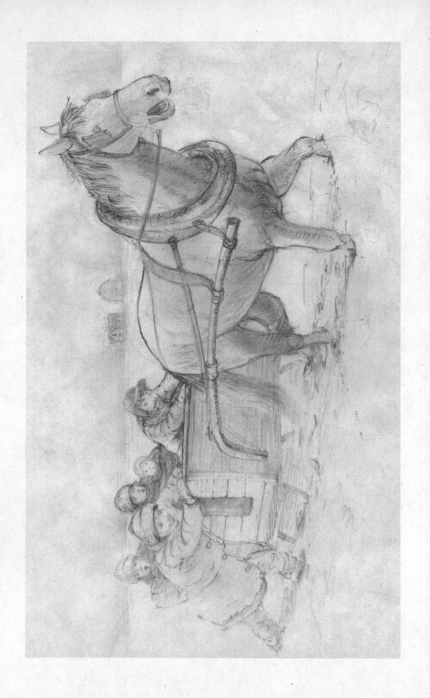

no one spoke again. But Mother laughed once, a small tickling sound that Mary hadn't heard for months.

The drifts grew deeper as they slid down into the wide valley where their farm lay. Then, after miles of thudding hooves and ice particles stinging their faces, they reached the yard. They were home. The air moaned as the wind cut itself on fences and the nooks of their outbuildings. Mary and Judith hopped off into the drift closest to the house, a live drift that seemed to move up around their feet as they stepped down. Mother carried Joseph off.

Papa led Clyde away. The old horse tottered on sweat-streaked legs, but still dragged the cutter with ears-forward eagerness.

Without a word of protest, Mary let herself be turned from the windy chaos of the yard and pulled inside through the back door. Suddenly tired, too tired even to take off her coat, she fell asleep in a chair by the cold stove.

She awoke in her bed, and the first thing she did was wiggle her toes, all warm under the covers. She counted each of them, up to ten. The roof sloped above her and the window shuddered in the occasional blast of wind. Mary wondered if Christmas had come yet. The tiny dormer window let in some light. It must be morning.

Then she remembered. They'd already been to church. Or at least they'd been to the school that, next year, doctor willing, she would attend. They hadn't stayed for church, but had come home in a rush because of the weather. The light above was evening light, not morning. Mary sighed. Someday soon she'd have a part in the Christmas program, as Judith had that very morning. Except she'd be Mary, not some foolish hiccuping sheep. Maybe Joseph would be her husband in the program, if he was tall enough by then.

Then she remembered her shoes. They'd be waiting for her downstairs under the tree! Throwing back the covers, she saw she was still dressed from the morning at school. Judith and Joseph were asleep. She ran down the stairs into the front room.

Three parcels lay under the tree, and the nativity scene had been set up there too with its ceramic animals and strangely dressed people. Two of the presents were big enough to be shoes.

Papa sat at one end of the sofa, reading a newspaper. He leaned toward the thin light offered by the frosted-up front window. He was using all his fingers to hold together the newspaper's many torn flaps. At the sofa's other end, Mother sat knitting with a bright blue yarn that looked like the yarn from a baby sweater Grandma had made for Joseph when he was a newborn, just before she died.

"The *Leader* says before the crash we produced forty percent of the world's wheat. Wasn't that a time!" Papa leaned his head back, dreamed a moment and aimed a wry grin at Mary. "Forty percent of the world's grasshoppers

32

now." Picking up the paper again, he mumbled, "Might as well feed the hoppers, I suppose. Can't sell the goldarn grain anyway."

Mother put down her knitting, frowned, picked it up again.

He read on, his lips moving painstakingly over the words. His lips moved when he read because Grandpa had made him quit school early to help on the farm. Mary had never met Grandpa, but she knew that he and Grandma had come from Holland, a place so far away that you had to travel across an ocean by ship. It was a place where people wore wooden shoes.

"Hitler is making it warm in Europe," said Papa. "He's got the German farmers producing most of their own food now. Guaranteed prices. No wonder we can't sell our grain! Says he'd like some more land."

"Wouldn't we all," said Mother, measuring with a long index finger. Then her needles clicked on. The presents were far from her mind and his too. "That man'll want ours next and welcome."

"Like to see him try. Even if it is a dust bowl," muttered Papa. "Goldarn paper!" Two halves of a page had come apart in his hands.

He looked imploringly at Mother, and she actually giggled.

"What I'd give for a new one, or at least one every farmer

'tween here and Regina hasn't spilt on, stood on and sat on." The pieces hung to his knees. "Maybe we ought to get us a wireless. Keep up that way. Radio is the voice of the future, Johnson says. Lots happening out in the wide world these days. What do you think?"

"We can't afford it after...you know." Mother's knitting became rough and jerky, and Mary knew this was not a good time to ask whether Saint Nicholas had happened by with new shoes. It was obvious that Black Peter had stayed away: All the packages were too big to be lumps of coal. "You know how we spent all the money, and that's that."

Papa sighed. "Don't let's get into that again," he said. "You did the best you could, Ruth. You had to have those drugs. And the doc wasn't sure it would hold..."

The needles had stopped clicking altogether. Papa fell silent too.

They were searching for words about the little angel Mother had lost, a baby who was born dead back when Judith had started this school year. This angel had gobbled up all the candy money and a lot of the shopping money. How did a lost baby have anything to do with money? There must be more to it, Mary reasoned. But she sure wasn't going to ask about that now. That topic always brought everyone's spirits crashing down. She didn't want to spoil what was left of Christmas. She understood that money was low, and her chances of getting shoes were even

34

lower. But then, Christmas was magic too. Anything could happen. She sat on a stool and threw out her feet, imagining the fine comfort of her shiny new shoes.

"Johnson says he'll swap a kit radio for milk."

They were moving on from the angel topic, then, but only to adult interests. Mary grew fidgety. Why did she always have to wait? Wait for school, wait for Christmas, wait for shoes, wait through small talk. "Papa!" she whined.

He leaned forward. "Did you want something, honey?" He began winking and smiling the way he used to do when they all went to town and each of the children was allowed a small but private stash of candy.

"Not till the others come down." Mother's face was firm as stone. And don't try changing her mind on this, the furrowed brow warned. Her needles clicked on again.

Knowing how much any argument had won her in the past—exactly nothing—Mary drifted off to the kitchen. She sat by the warm stove and waved her finger through the steam jetting up out of the kettle. Hearing a rattle at the window, she rose to have a look. A single tiny bare spot showed large drops of rain falling, with balls of ice mixed in for good measure. "Papa, it's raining!"

He came in and performed an exaggerated squint out the window. Picking up Mary, he let her kneel on the counter for a better view. He took a flat-ended wooden spoon from a nail on the wall and scraped away a swath of soft frost.

"Chinook," he said. "There's a wind clear from the Pacific coast. Old Clyde couldn't pull in this nohow."

"We were smart to get ourselves home then," Mary said.

"I figured this morning it had warmed up a tad."

"Good." Mother's voice came unexpectedly from the other side of Papa's head. "At least now we can move."

"Move?" Papa sounded worried.

"Take the buggy to town now and again."

"Oh. That would be nice, Ruthie, but if it thaws out too early, the road will be a mire. As for a melt being good, we need to keep this snow. Bare dirt just dries out and blows away, as I think we all know by now."

"I'm hoping for a good rainy spring," she said. "And I want to get out." Mary remembered that Mother used to be adventurous, driving to town by herself. But other than this morning, she hadn't left the farm in months.

"Me too."

Then Mother's hand was up by Mary's face, resting on Papa's shoulder. The fingers were long and tapered, though badly chapped. Mary had never really noticed them before. Mary inspected her fingers, which by comparison were smooth and stubby, with dirty nails.

"What are you looking at?" Papa asked, hugging her swiftly.

"Just checking if my hands are nice like Mother's." Mary

looked again, but the hand was gone, its tapered and veined beauty tucked bashfully into an apron pocket.

Papa smiled. "She always had nice hands, our pretty young Ruth did."

Mother pulled away. Both hands stuffed into her pockets, she walked to the foot of the stairs, calling, "Judith! Joseph! You won't sleep tonight if you don't get up now!" She returned to her knitting in the front room.

Chapter 5

Within minutes of being called, Judith and Joseph tumbled down the stairs. Joseph ran to the tree and stooped to investigate a ceramic camel with a missing leg. Then, remembering his mission, he pounced on the parcels and brought them eagerly to Mother. He shouted, "What one's mine? What one's mine? Mine!"

Judith tried to snatch the presents from Mother's lap, but Mother placed her hand on them, looked up and asked, "Is this how we receive gifts from each other?"

"No, ma'am," said Judith, blushing. "May I?"

Mother handed the presents to Judith. Studying the label on the first one, she read aloud, "M...A...." Eyes averted, Judith tossed it back onto Mother's lap. Then she read another, "J...U...D...I...T...H. That leaves this one for you."

She didn't look at Joseph as she extended her arm to hand him the last package. He clutched it to his chest and stepped back, plainly expecting his oldest and meanest sister to change her mind. Just as his hand came down to rip the brown paper wrapping, Mother said, "Not so fast, young man. First we'll have the star and the story."

"Aawwh!"

"We all heard the story this morning," said Papa. "Do we really need it again?"

Mother raised her eyebrows, one at a time, like she was weighing the merits of his point: the usual good of children being made to wait for no reason whatsoever against the immediate peace of their gratification, in this case, unwrapping presents. "All right," she replied. "But we still have the star to put on first. Who will do that?"

Judith and Joseph both galloped to the tree. "I will! I will!"

Papa asked, "How 'bout you, Mary?"

Mary pointed at Joseph. "Let him do it."

Looking at Judith, Papa lifted his eyebrows.

"Draw straws," she answered.

"Is it so all-fired important?"

Judith's bottom lip came out. "Yes."

Sighing, Papa pulled three green needles from the tree. He arranged them behind his back, then displayed them between his thumb and forefinger. "Try yer luck, ladies and gent!"

Joseph chose a needle, and Judith did too. Mary took the

last one and when they held them up, hers was longest. Papa picked her up and carried her to the tree, but she wiggled and kicked her legs. "No. No! I want Joseph to do it!"

As Papa set her down, Mary glanced over at Judith, who glared back at her. Mary sighed. As always, she would pay a price for Judith not winning the contest. Judith never forgot a slight.

Joseph was formally given the star by Mother and carried, squealing with joy and getting a whisker rub on his baby neck, toward the tree. Papa lifted him high and Joseph placed the star's green tin cone over the topmost stem. The star glittered. Its five arms were covered in sparkles that reflected any light that came their way. For the past two years, Mary had placed it. Judith brushed by and used her needle to leave a red scratch on Mary's hand. Still, Mary felt glad Joseph had set the star up high and glad that Judith had not.

Finally it was time. They were allowed to rip into the paper wrappings. Joseph cheered at the sight of a small wooden mallet. He immediately began to hammer the floor. Judith, slower in getting to her present, eventually uncovered a pair of shoes. Although they had been buffed up, Mary could see wear marks in their leather uppers. They were used.

"Thank you," Judith said, without enthusiasm.

"You're welcome," Mother answered.

Mary's present didn't feel right. It was too soft. And Judith's new scuffed shoes meant one thing: no money. Could there possibly be two sets of shoes if Judith's pair was used?

In that moment Mary's shoes vanished, sucked back into the world of daydreams.

Mary swallowed and made a show of reading the newsprint wrapped around her present. But as nobody seemed to pay any attention to her, she went ahead and ripped the paper. A dark painted eye gazed up at her. Mary looked at Papa, who was smiling broadly. Mother smiled too, smiled as she had not done for some time, smiled even though she had practically promised new shoes for Christmas. A sense of quiet panic stole up Mary's throat. Hot tears began to form. She forced them away.

The present she'd waited for so patiently all these months turned out to be a doll, not un-Judith shoes. Mary closed her prickly eyes and opened them to the awful sight of Judith grinning at her.

Mother smiled sadly. "I didn't think a nosebag would do the trick."

Papa's eager face had relaxed into disappointment.

Mary looked at her mother and her father. She tried to smile. She knew they had done their best, but knowing that didn't make it any easier. She'd got nothing but an old nosebag.

She bolted upstairs, hid under the bed covers and cried, asking over and over why nothing ever went right for her. Later, drained of tears, she felt foolish. Why had she imagined there would be money for shoes when they had to do without the simplest everyday things like tea? She sighed and unwrapped her present anyway.

It was a doll, but not a real one with porcelain hands and feet and face and lacy clothes like Judith's. This doll was canvas and naked. Two crude arms and two crude legs stuck out into the air as if stretching to recover lost hands and feet. Its seams were evenly stitched, but with a fine black thread. The white-painted but expressionless face had large black spots for eyes, lips of red paint, and hair of black paint. The paint was still sticky. It was a nosebag with no nose. Who could feel anything for such a doll?

And worse, when fall came, she would have to go to school in Judith's annoying old shoes. With cracks. No, I won't! she vowed angrily. I'll go barefoot first!

Then she thought of the ride in to the play that morning, how cozy it had been, how full of hope. Her parents always did the best they could, she told herself. If the Christmas money had been spent on other things, nobody was at fault, unless they blamed that little angel Mother had lost last fall. She looked at the doll again and propped it up against the pillow. With a face like that, the doll could use a friend. When the doll fell over, she sat it back up. When the light disappeared from the window, Mary took the doll downstairs.

"I'm sorry, Mary," said Papa as Mary sat on the bottom step. "There was no money left to buy a nice one."

"Nor shoes," said Mother. "Maybe next year."

Judith sat between Papa and Mother, holding her feet out in her new shoes. "I think they do fit well, Mother. They're oh so comfortable." She raised her lip at Mary.

Just then Joseph whacked Papa's foot with the mallet.

"Ow! Joseph, by gum and by golly, you go over there and fix yer jalopy, will ya?"

"I didn't buy a thing for you," Mary confessed, ignoring Judith.

"Well, it's not much, I know." Papa pointed Joseph off to a far corner, picked up his foot to rub it and faced Mary appealingly. "We made her while you kids slept."

No kidding, thought Mary. "No, Papa. I love her. Is it a he or a she?"

"He."

"She, as anyone can see." Mother peeked up from beneath lowered brows.

Mary put her face against the doll's cold, coarse face. "And what is my baby's name?"

Papa glanced at the nativity scene and smiled mischievously. "Jessy."

"Don't be sacrilegious, Raynold," Mother scolded.

"Jessy is sacrilegious?"

"We all know what you're getting at."

He smiled guiltily, as if he'd been caught in a lie. "Okay, but it's not so far from the stable to a nosebag. Pretty darn close, if you ask me."

Mary looked up to the yellow angel on the ceiling and remembered their deal. She had given up her shoes. Would she get the peace and quiet she had asked for in return?

Mother fussed with her knitting, brushing Judith's hand away as she picked at the pretty blue wool.

"Jessy. Hmm." Mary liked the feel of that name. Ignoring the disapproval in Mother's eye, she dandled the doll on her knee. She thought the face looked a bit happier now that everyone knew her name. "Maybe Jessy needs to go to bed for a while," said Mary, "even though she didn't do anything wrong yet."

Papa was smiling as Mary turned to go back upstairs, but Judith was not.

"Whatever you call her, she'll need some clothes," said Mother. She lifted her knitting proudly. Her nice blue-lined hand held up a small blue wool dress, half finished. "Put her to bed for now, Mary, and in the morning I hope she'll be fit to be seen."

Mary ran upstairs, put Jessy to bed and bustled around her. Jessy felt cold, her head was not comfortable on the pillow and she even came down with a sudden fever. One

44

moment passed into another, and Mary had to be called down to supper. Only then did she realize how frozen she felt. When she came down into the kitchen, she ran to Papa, just returning from evening chores. He dripped with sleet and carried a pail of frothy milk. Mary hugged him earnestly. "Thank you, Papa, for Jessy." She ran to Mother and hugged her. "Thank you, Mother, for making Jessy's dress."

"You're welcome." Mother pulled away from Mary to plunk a bowl down in the center of the kitchen table. For this evening only, the table's stained wood and scars were hidden under a cover of linen. That single white sheet, spotless, transformed the kitchen into a marvellously festive and happy place.

When they were all sitting down and examining the collection of bowls before them, Mother said, "Mary, will you kindly say grace?"

Feeling solemn, Mary folded her hands and bowed her head. This was usually Judith's job, and she felt every eye must be on her. "Thank you, God," she said, "for sending us our little friends. Ah-men." When Mary looked up again, Papa had a lopsided grin on his face. Mother's cheek was twitching. Joseph was flying his fork through the air like a bird. But across the steaming bowls, Judith glared at Mary.

It was a fancy meal, with cabbage and carrot soup, chicken, potatoes (mashed on this very special day), a squash and turnip dish that Mary couldn't decide if she liked, bread, milk for the children and tea for Mother and Papa. For dessert, Mother set a candied apple on each plate.

Even Judith found it within herself to smile at such a treat.

Chapter 6

Mary woke up as the blankets were moving toward the door. It had to be Judith, up to her old tricks. Angrily, Mary flipped herself over to protest and found herself looking straight into Judith's eyes, a moody gray like Mother's. The blankets crept on.

Judith put out her hand to touch Jessy, who lay on the bed between them. Jessy, completely at home, gazed up at the ceiling. How had she come to be there? Mary remembered laying the doll on her other side, the side away from Judith. Now she grabbed the doll and turned away before Judith could injure her. Mary received a long hard pinch on her shoulder. But she said nothing. Better to stay quiet than have Judith add a punch as well.

"Joseph," said Judith, rolling off her side of the bed. "You'll put the blankets back on the bed right now, if you know what's good for you."

Joseph huffed and puffed around the bed, threw the blankets in a heap on top of Mary, peeked in at Jessy, who lay in the crook of Mary's arm, and meekly followed his sister downstairs. The room became peaceful and quiet. Mary set Jessy's head on her pillow. The doll's friendly black eyes were full of understanding.

Mary, warming now under the blankets, recalled once again how last week she had placed Jessy on the bed and left her. It had started as an experiment, more or less, but ended as a disaster. She just wanted to see if Judith could at least be friendly when no one was looking. Was that a week after Christmas, or two? Time was hard to keep track of after days of being kept indoors. Wrapped in a blanket, Mary had hidden in the wardrobe and waited for Judith to come upstairs and change after school. Judith came into the room, leaned down, looked around and pinched Jessy. She pinched a doll!

"Caught you red-handed!" Mary had shouted as she sprang out of the wardrobe. "What's the matter with you anyway?"

"Just seeing what this rag is made of, you poisonous little brat."

"If I'm so poisonous, why are you pinching a doll?"

"You're so right," Judith said, pinching Mary hard on the arm.

Mary had grabbed Jessy and run downstairs, crying to Papa and pointing at the new red welt. Papa glanced at her arm, kept shoving firewood into the heater and called Judith down. "What's this all about? You know you're not supposed to get her riled up and running around, what with her condition."

Judith told her story.

"You keep your fingers apart from that doll," Papa said after she finished.

"Yes, sir." Judith stared at the floor and kicked a building block into the corner.

Mother, listening at the kitchen doorway, added, "And you, Mary, you don't set your sister up for trouble that way. That's a mean trick to play."

"Yes, ma'am."

Since then Judith had missed few chances to pinch and annoy, but now the pinches were delivered to Mary's back and legs, places where the evidence of cruelty was not easily noticed. But Judith had pinched a doll! What kind of monster would do that? She sighed. This was why Jessy slept on the other side. And this meant Mary had to sleep closer to the monster herself. But then Jessy could lie at a distance, safe and sound. How had Jessy ever got between them on the bed? Mary picked up the doll and hugged her. "Oh, Jessy," she said, "you will have to watch out for Judith. You know she can't be trusted."

The doll seemed to agree, but also not agree. What could Jessy mean by that? Thinking of the weeks following

Christmas, Mary found she couldn't remember much in Judith's favor. But setting aside the torments of her sister, the days melted and merged and hung in the past like a pleasant haze at sunrise. She sighed happily.

A strange noise came through the door. It took a moment for Mary to realize Mother was humming downstairs. Was that a Christmas carol? As they listened, Mary held Jessy out to hear the song:

What child is this, who, laid to rest,
On Mary's lap is sleeping?
Whom angels greet with anthems sweet
While shepherds watch are keeping?

Mary smiled. Mother hadn't sung anything since last summer, when her lost angel had squeezed all the music out of her. And while it wasn't exactly a happy-sounding song, it did have angels in it. Mary felt sure this meant life on the farm must get better now.

"You may not agree with me," said Mary, "but it's because of you, Jessy, my girl, that our long wide white valley is forgetting how to be sad.

"Shall we go out and do the chores, my dear? Yes we shall. A storm last week and cold every day and Judith non-stop, of course, but we have each other." Mary sighed dramatically. "How about we play mother and baby today and help Papa with the chores tonight? Tonight we shall have to be out of the way before the nasty monster comes home." She hugged the doll again and set her down gently.

"Aren't you cold, Jessy, dear? I do think I must have taken a chill, and we may have to go to town for the doctor. You'll likely be next, poor thing. Like to go down to the front room and look out at the valley?"

Jessy's round rough face indicated that she was all for a trip down the stairs, so Mary wrapped her carefully in her blanket. The blanket was a gift, not to Mary but to Jessy, a worn terry-velvet towel that Mother said was pretty near all that was left of better days. Suddenly shivering with cold, Mary grabbed Jessy and ran down the stairs to the front room. Joseph lay on the floor there, contemplating a new fortress built out of blocks. But that room was cold too, so she went into the kitchen instead. She plunked Jessy down on a chair near the black, smoke-smelling cookstove.

"Not too cold, not too hot, just right," said Mary. "Better enjoy yourself while you can, dear, because all too soon the nasty monster will be home."

"You really could be nicer to Judith," Mother said. She was peeling a huge potato. A long bumpy tail of potato skin was winding like a snake about her arm.

Mary wondered about Mother's change of personality. She seemed less angry now than a few weeks ago. What had happened? She could hardly ask something so personal. "I heard you singing," she said instead.

Mother didn't smile exactly, but she didn't frown either. "Life goes on. And people rely on me." She looked over with those gloomy gray eyes of hers.

"Like me."

"Like you."

"Jessy too." Jessy took a bow, and Mary grinned at her.

"I'm just saying we're all in this together. Why not make the best of it?"

Mary tucked Jessy under her arm. "We'd rather be alone, Mother. Judith's always pinching or getting us into trouble. She doesn't know how to treat company."

"Well, your words hurt her. You both could use a friend. This dust bowl is a lonesome place."

"She doesn't want to be my friend."

"Everyone wants friends."

If Judith wanted a friendship, thought Mary, her pinching fingers sure didn't seem very inclined to help out. Mary snapped her own fingers in the air.

Mother looked at her sharply over another potato, and Mary lowered her fingers.

Mother sighed. "Why don't you go find a story to read?" she said.

Mary felt she would rather go out to the barn to help Papa. She often poured slop for the pig, whose hungry and inquisitive little ones she loved to stroke. Maybe she'd gather eggs. The huddled party of red chickens bickered and gossiped ceaselessly in a dusty corner of their cold run, but even in winter a few of them took a break from their busy social lives to lay an egg or two. Mary pulled the egg basket from under the bench. She planned also to throw hay to the cow and her fawn-brown calf, and pet the ever-patient Clyde. Today she had to stay clear of his huge stamping hooves. Only last week, Papa had been very short with her for not paying attention to where she was going.

"Can we go out to the barn?"

"No, better not. It's so cold out there. Why don't you find a story to read to your brother? Keep him busy. You're good at keeping people busy. But first eat your porridge."

"Aw. Jessy wants to help with chores." And although she read stories very well and enjoyed pictures, Mary wanted action, not to sit through a book. "Besides, Papa needs me. He said I can help out any time I want."

"What did we agree about the nice blue dress going out to that filthy barn?" Mother pointed at Jessy with the paring knife.

"But I have to go out."

"You want to catch that pretty wool I knitted on slivers and nails?"

Mary leaned down to listen to Jessy, who told her it was no use getting angry because Mother had made up her mind. And warmer days were coming. "What's that? Oh, all right. Jessy says we are hungry after all, and to stay home, so I guess after breakfast we'll read *Old Nursery Stories and Rhymes*. She really likes the 'Goldilocks' story." Mary placed the doll in the egg basket and swung it around her head for a balloon ride. "Joseph can be the audience if he behaves himself and doesn't yell every minute."

That night Judith was particularly vicious, delivering a kick that left three wide scratches on Mary's calf. Mary hopped out of bed and limped downstairs crying, "Mother, Judith keeps pinching and pushing and kicking. Look at this. I can't take it anymore!"

Mother and Papa sat in the warm kitchen, which rang with pops and snaps as knots of burning wood exploded in the stove. Mother sighed and said, "Will you go up, or shall I?"

"You go."

Papa seemed to be piecing together an odd contraption. There were many parts spread out on the table, all intriguing and none familiar. "What are you doing, Papa?" Mary asked.

Papa was concentrating. Surrounded by wires and spools, he said nothing.

"Did something else get broken?"

"Putting a kit together."

"A lunch kit?"

"Does this look like lunch?"

"No. But what…"

"A wireless."

"Where'd you get it?"

"Remember the milk and packages of cheese that go in with Judith?" He peered down to examine some intricate parts. "I don't know about this fine work."

Mary nodded at the back of his bent head. "Uh-huh."

"Johnson from the co-op sent it out in trade for the milk and cheese. They call it a kit because you put the pieces together yourself. Don't touch that iron, by the way. It's hot enough to melt ya like butter."

She jerked back her hand. Though she knew better, she had almost touched the iron. She studied Papa quickly to see if he'd noticed. He hadn't. "Why?"

"Got to melt the solder to hold the bits together."

Mary sat on a chair to watch him. He twisted together two wires and laid them on the iron. When he touched them with the wire of solder, the wires sucked the glistening metal into their winding strands. A few drops of molten silver trickled down the side of the iron. He checked the directions again, pursing his lips.

Holding the page close to the flickering candle and squinting, Papa moved his lips, soundlessly concentrating on the words. Judith's lips moved like that when she claimed to be reading. Mary expected that next year when she went to school, she would do likewise. No, she decided, her lips certainly would not move like that mean old Judith's did.

Returning from upstairs, Mother sat down by Mary. "You can go up now."

Mary climbed the stairs, expecting the worst.

Back in bed, there was a strange sniffling under the blankets. "You always get everything," Judith whispered quietly, as if it was all she could manage to get out.

Mary recalled the shoes again. She hadn't thought of the new shoes for weeks, having been so busy with Jessy. She didn't care about shoes now. She stroked Jessy's face in the cold darkness of the bedroom, feeling places where the rough old canvas smoothed out. The doll was wearing thin in spots. She looked old already, unlike Judith's doll, who always looked new. A hard push now could tear Jessy's skin. "You got the shoes. I got the nosebag."

Judith snorted. "Shows what you know. Selfish pig."

Mary touched Jessy's face gently. Even in the night she could picture it, darkening with ashes and grime. The doll fell to the floor often. She made excursions to the barn, in secret of course, where she landed in the dust and straw and worse. Jessy meant so much to her. The black round eyes were surprised at nothing and at everything. Jessy was the first real friend Mary had ever known. And she was good at games too, even if Mary had to supply Jessy with hands and feet. She hugged Jessy. "How I love you," she whispered.

"What?"

"Nothing."

Something tiny lay on the bed between the sheets. It was long and had pointy ends. Mary popped it into her mouth and chewed. It tasted like an oat. She often chewed oats while standing at Clyde's head, if she could snitch some before he slobbered on the lot. Mary wondered why Judith had brought oats to bed, then realized the oat must have come from Jessy. The doll was stuffed with oats. Mary smiled: How smart Papa was at making things.

She heard another sniffle but didn't say a word to Judith. With the mood her sister was in that night, why ask for trouble? Judith was welcome to sniffle all she liked. Because of Judith, Mary had done more than her share of sniffling.

Chapter 7

A few days later, the morning stampede into the kitchen was halted by a new presence, a new sound in the air. The children slid to a standstill. The new sound came from the table, where a small box hissed and popped. Papa stood beside it, grinning. Bending over, he dialed a couple of knobs this way and that way.

Mother was adding milk to her flapjack batter. Papa twirled the dials and watched the gentle swing of her hips. A trace of a grin played about her face too. Her body was turned away from the noise and action around the table. Papa released the knobs.

Closest to the box was Joseph. He reached a pudgy hand up to one of the knobs. Quick as a hen striking a seed, Papa slapped the hand away. Joseph drew back his hand with equal speed. Rubbing his knuckles absently, he said, "But why, Papa? What is it?"

"This is not a toy for you children to play with." Papa looked at each of them in turn, wagging his finger sternly.

"Isn't that the truth?" said Mother. "This is your father's toy. Make sure you let him play with it." She looked out the window, which was clear, and went back to work with her wooden spoon.

"That's right," he said, nodding. "It's my toy. Mine. Get it?" But then Papa grinned. He never could remain stern for long.

A strange crackling sound kept leaking from the box. Papa fiddled with a dial. More noises came in, faded away, came back. The noises became a man's voice: "…walked up to me while I was speaking with my friend, Bill Aberhart, and this man says to me, 'Preacher, God is my field, all blown away. Everyone knows that but you.' But do you know that, radio friend? How can you blow away God?" The voice sputtered, faded out.

"Goldarn signal anyway." Papa turned the dials.

Then another voice: "And this just in. General Motors has capitulated to worker demands and recognized the United Auto Workers' union. This has occurred after a forty-four-day occupation of GM factories involving violent clashes between police and strikers, and the stationing of machine-gun nests in Flint, Michigan streets by the National Guard."

"Wash up and get ready to eat," Mother said.

Sighing, Papa spun the left knob till it clicked. The crackling stopped, and the unknown voices left the kitchen, leaving them all in a stunned silence.

Mary had been holding Jessy up to let her see Papa's new toy, and he looked the doll full in her dirty face. "Well, Jessy," he said with a smirk, "you've come into quite a world. The people are either being gunned down to save a few measly bucks on wages, or they're pleading with heaven to end all their troubles. Both great solutions, let me tell you."

"Raynold," said Mother, pouring warm water into a basin, "don't infect the children."

"The day our troubles end is the day this here doll wakes up and helps out with chores." Papa looked at Mary more fiercely than she was used to. "I mean really helps out, not just pretend."

Were they planning to fight again? Mary hoped not. Papa tapped the box, drumming his big blunt fingertips on it. The hissing sound started again. The children studied the noisy box intently. What would it say now?

Papa laughed. "That's Mother's pan, not the radio, you silly kittens!"

Sure enough, a spoonful of batter had dropped into the hot grease of the frying pan. The children smiled at him sheepishly.

"You weren't always such a cynic," Mother said wearily.

More than a tinge of sadness showed in the slump of her shoulders.

Papa washed and dried his hands and sat down. He rubbed his eyes with his palms, and Mary studied the very large veins in his square hands. "At least I'm not doing myself in, am I, like some have." He grabbed the pitcher and poured milk into all the children's glasses. Judith scowled because she usually poured her own. "There's a thing, now. A drought always gets you a good crop of suicides, at least."

"Maybe we haven't lost as much as them."

"No, but maybe we haven't kept enough to get by neither. Six, seven years ago we made five hundred dollars a year. Less than a hundred now. I hate to think how much less."

"The times will turn." Mother's words were firm, but her voice had that tone again that Mary hadn't heard since Christmas. "Until then, we've got the eggs and milk to keep us afloat."

"Not at sixty cents to the bushel. And not if we don't get a crop. No, Ruthie, times won't turn!" Papa still held up the jug, oblivious to this weight that Mary could hardly lift.

Those big veins in Papa's arms and hands looked like the wrought-iron steps of the old buggy. Mary knew by experience that they were hard too. Why did his hands look like tree roots and Mother's stay slender, although red and chapped? Was outside work so hard that it turned a man's hands to roots? She studied Joseph's baby arms and hands. Had Papa's arms ever been so smooth? The next time they saw Johnson, she decided, she would check to see if his hands were hard as roots too, or if it was just Papa.

Before long, Mother set the first steaming flapjacks on the table. "Well, look at this: We can feed ourselves. We're not on Relief like some of our neighbors. That's something, isn't it?"

Every few weeks, usually when he'd seen a public notice that potatoes could be picked up at such and such a place, Papa would flutter and shake his out-of-date newspaper and swear he'd never take Relief. A government handout wasn't something to be ashamed of, he said, but it wouldn't chase away your troubles either. Now he frowned, forked a flapjack onto his plate, added a dollop of butter and, looking down at his plate, said, "I'm thinking of joining the CCF. They'll get us a decent market. Then we'll only have to worry about getting us a crop to sell."

"Mary, don't play with your food," Mother said.

Mary stopped burbling her milk. "What's a CCF?" she asked as white bubbles popped all the way from her lip to her nose.

Papa gazed at his plate, deep in thought. "And don't go telling me what I used to say about running with lemmings, neither," he said finally. "Us in a good market—that's all I care about."

"I'll run with lemons, Papa," Joseph said eagerly.

"Lemmings, not lemons. And if you do, you'll have to jump off a cliff."

"Maybe I'll just stay here then." Joseph shoved a finger into a flapjack.

"Cooperative Commonwealth Federation," Judith announced. She turned toward Mother as if awaiting some reward for this tardy information.

"Whatever makes you happy," said Mother, seating herself. "Judith, grace."

"God is great, God is good. Let us thank him for our food."

Except for Joseph smacking his lips, they ate their meal in silence. Judith had said the right words, Mary was sure. The food was good. Nobody had done the least bit of wrong. There did not seem to be any reason for such silence.

After breakfast all three children went out to the barn to watch their father muck out the pigsty. It was a muddy Saturday, and warm. Mary allowed Jessy to come but held onto her tight. They were playing in a sunny protected spot between the open barn doors when Papa came out, pushing the wheelbarrow. He set it down, leaned against a big doorpost, breathed deeply and shoved his hands in behind the bib of his overalls.

"See, Jessy?" Mary ran her fingers along the bulging veins on Papa's forearms. She felt Jessy's smooth arms. "Isn't it a lovely day, Papa?"

"Sure is, sweetheart," he said. "Though I think by the looks of that sky, we're about done with this lovely spell."

"And we need that snow back quick, right, Papa?" Judith asked. Copying his actions, she leaned on the door. She raised up her face to gape at him.

"Yup. Sure do." He scoured the sky overhead.

"Why's that sky so yellow?" Mary asked. Not that it was so very yellow this morning, but Mary wanted to hear her father talk. Despite his anger at the drought, Papa liked to tell her about the prairie turning to dust and rising over itself like a great yellow ghost. When he described drying sloughs and creeks and the homeless waterfowl and the parched land broken by huge cracks and the hot wind-blown dirt collecting in summer drifts behind every fence-post and rock, Mary saw it all more clearly than she ever did in real life. Now, with all this wet mud around them, Papa might tell her the story of dry dirt, which was jailed in ice every winter, then released in spring to drift and wiggle and creep toward the house with one intention: to foil Mother's best housekeeping efforts.

But Papa only sighed. "You been told why your whole life, young lady."

"I forgot."

"How I wish you could see an honest-to-goodness blue sky for once."

Mary looked over at Judith, whose eager face was drooping. Her eyes were falling away from Papa's uplifted face. Worse, Judith had the beginnings of that look. She'd be in a monster mood tonight. And Mary had done nothing to deserve it.

"Train!" Joseph called. A faint moan came down from the western edge of their shallow valley. Only Joseph paid attention to it.

"Why aren't you happy, Papa?" asked Mary. "Is it the Depression?" She'd heard this word often. Usually given by Mother as the reason for people's misfortunes, it was an all-purpose word, good for anything from blights of grasshoppers to moments of sadness.

Papa glanced down at her and said, "I'm not sure you'd understand." He looked up at the sky and smiled sadly. "When Judith was born..."

Judith jerked her head up.

He watched a raven flap across the sky. "Well, things looked not so bad back then. But we already lost our first baby. I mean, Mother made an angel, and we lost her. This is hard to describe to someone like you. You've never been betrayed, Meadow Muffin. The next year was the year before the big crash, and Judith was born. Anybody with open eyes could see that things had to go sour, not that

I saw. You were born out here. Opa died and we buried him in town. We lost our savings on October 29. Then we found out about the hole in your heart. There seemed to be no end to what a man could lose, and that was just the beginning."

"I know what a crash is," Judith said. The small knowing grin on her face told Mary this would be a joke of some kind, or a trick.

Mary didn't know. She suspected, though, that crash and depression had practically the same meaning. But she wasn't going to ask and give Judith any satisfaction.

Joseph swung on the handle of the heavily loaded wheelbarrow. He had a single intention: to tip the wheelbarrow and spill the pig manure, which reeked and dripped through the plank sides. Judith, done waiting for anyone to ask her what a crash might be, kicked at the barn door. When Papa remained lost in his reflections, she ran out into the yard to stand by the iron pump at the well.

Papa thought for a moment, then fingered his knee, where the patch was coming loose. "Then I got me a hole in my heart too, somehow, and lost what little faith I had. Watch out, son!" The wheelbarrow was ready to spill as its legs sank into the soft soil. "Can't you leave that manure alone? Go help Judith, will you?" Papa pulled Joseph off the handle, shook his head sternly and moved the dripping reeking mess to solid ground. Leaning against the doorpost again, he added, "A crash, by the way, is what we're living here. When you lose your shirt, and nobody's interested because they lost theirs too."

"Will we crash again, Papa?" Mary asked.

"Can't say." He scanned the yard till his eyes rested on Judith. "I guess we ought to get ourselves uncrashed first."

Judith was filling a pail with water, pumping at a pump handle as high as her head. Its metallic squealing filled the yard.

"It ain't right," whispered Papa, "but every time I look at her I see a parade of all the things I lost." He spoke as if he were telling Mary a secret, and a thrill ran through her at his new, confidential tone.

Releasing the handle, Judith turned to the right. She raised her arm. With her palm up and fingers extended, she might have been summoning someone nobody else could see.

Chapter 8

"Guess I'm not much of a father," said Papa, sighing again. "We should have moved away, up north or off to the coast with all them Joneses and Smiths. They knew when to leave." He walked away from the barn, his rubber boots slurping and sucking in the mucky yard. Past the lean-to, his head turned to see what Judith had found to point at.

"Two-bottom plow to the northwest," he called back. Mary and Joseph ran out to see for themselves. A huge black cloud that did look like a plow hovered there. Its two black tines scraped along the skyline, plowing a path toward them. Ropes of lightning hung like a harness from its sharp points. A low growl of thunder rushed over the steaming brown land.

"Papa!" exclaimed Joseph. "I just saw thunder, and it looks like lightning!"

"You see lightning," said Judith, scowling at Mary, "and you hear thunder."

"The Doerksens will be getting her now," said Papa, "and I guess there'll be plenty left for us all to see and hear both. You children dash in quick and tell Mother a big storm is on the way and that I say to batten the hatches."

They ran into the house. Mother, beginning the laundry, was emptying a pail of hot water into the washtub. "Mom," asked Judith, "what's batten the hatches?"

"Why?"

"Dad says a big storm is coming and to batten them now."

"Goodness me, it's always something," moaned Mother. "Mary, you take Joseph and close the north shutters. Judith, you take the west ones." Mother ran for the stairs.

Mary set Jessy down in her place at the table, grabbed Joseph's hand and pulled him out the door. They ran to the box under the north window and climbed up on it. Thunder ran everywhere in long loud peals, like the bell in town when it called everyone to church. The thunder boomed as they undid the latches and wrestled the shutters away from the wall. They had to fight the wind. What had always been an easy chore seemed to take a long time.

The wind changed direction, and the second shutter shut with a bang. Mary turned each center latch securely, the way she'd been taught. She heard Mother slamming shutters and windows upstairs. When they were nearly done, they heard banging from the west side. That had to be Judith at work. Mary sent Joseph to help Judith and ran to the barn to help Papa.

Papa was just closing the big doors, which swung in the wind. Mary held one. The door was warped and jiggling and hard to hold. He brought the doors together and forced a bar down into the wooden yokes. The cracks in the doors let through bars of sunlight, smudged yellow from the mingled dust high in the sky. The light flickered and was gone.

A cold gust swept into the yard and whined through the darkened barn. A drumming began on the roof, as from thousands of nervous fingers. Mary ran to look out the small door. The hail cascaded down all at once, as if someone had tripped and spilt a barrow-load of ice marbles onto their farm. Mary's hand found Papa's, and they watched the hail bounce off the sheds and fences and water pump, and blanket the yard and fields.

The temperature dropped quickly. As the rattling went on overhead, their breaths became visible. Laura the cow and Clyde the horse shuffled in their stalls. Stella grunted in her pigpen. As if hoping to escape notice in their corner, the chickens were silent. About fifteen minutes into the storm, Papa said, "Let's cross over in this lull." He picked up Mary, and away they went, out through the low door, rushing toward the house. The yard, pure mud minutes earlier, was now a sugary white, like creamy frosting on a birthday cake you knew was really chocolate inside. The wind tugged at them, and Papa's boots crunched the ice underfoot. His strong legs carried them to the kitchen stoop.

Papa closed the door on a thunderclap that shook the house to the floorboards. Every window rattled. The three children looked at each other. After Papa set her down, Mary ran to her seat at the table, yelling, "I'll have to show Jessy the storm." But the doll wasn't on her chair. "Come out, come out, wherever you are!" she called, but found no sign of Jessy beside the chair, either, nor under the table.

"Lose something?" Papa asked.

"Jessy's gone. I put her right here on my chair." Mary patted the cold wood of her chair seat. Another clap of thunder shook the kitchen and rumbled off toward the living room. Mary ran that way, thinking she could have been wrong. But Jessy was not there either. Nor was she in bed, in the wardrobes, under the sofa, in the cupboard, under the beds, on top of the wardrobes, behind the sofa, by the cupboard, in the firewood bin, in the butter churn.

Jessy had vanished.

Mary ran up to her room for the third time. Why did things always go wrong for her? she wondered in a fit of despair. She threw herself on the bed, crying on the same pillow she'd shared with Jessy only hours before.

"We'll find her," said Papa from the door. "In all the excitement you probably left her outside. I expect she's in the barn, honey."

"She's not in the barn."

"Well, tonight at chores I'll look the place over."

Mary calmed down. Papa was always right. And this time she wouldn't mind being wrong. She saw the sad eyes pleading for help; she saw Jessy swimming in the slop between the cow's back legs or gashed by Clyde's heavy metal shoes.

"Can't you look now, Papa?"

"I doubt she'll be going anywhere."

"Won't Jessy be eaten to death by one of the animals?"

"I guess she'll just give them some company out in the barn."

Overhead, fingers of wind caught at the eaves. They scratched at the house, tried to pry off the roof. Thunder broke again and again, rumbling, Mary could tell by the echo, way out over the prairie. It was comforting to have Papa's strong arms about her.

By evening the thunder had long since ceased, and the wind with it. Mary went out to the barn with Papa. Winter had returned. It was hard to believe winter had ever gone away. The snow lay deep as her knees in places. She had to struggle to keep up with Papa and his shiny tin pail. While he did the chores, she checked every nook she could find.

She found no sign of Jessy, not a scrap of canvas, not a tell-tale thread of blue yarn.

"Papa, I can't find her. Do animals eat wool?"

"A goat might. None of our animals would. Do some clear thinking about the last things you did together. Then you'll know where to look."

Mary tried to think clearly. Maybe while they were shuttering the house she had laid Jessy down. In that case her doll would be somewhere near the north window.

From the yellow circle of light thrown by the barn lantern, Mary ran out into the night, toward the house. A long white drift, higher than Mary's shoulder, lay under the north window. She dug in the snow for a while, kicking it aside. The snow was heavy, and she grew frustrated. She had no light. She had no idea where to begin. Crying bitterly, she went into the house, dejected, tired, cold and wet through.

Mary ate her supper in silence. Joseph smacked his food as usual, and Mother shushed him as usual. Judith was calm and quiet. Nobody seemed to have grasped the extent of the catastrophe, except perhaps Papa, who sent a few consoling looks Mary's way before turning on the radio and listening to Glenn Miller.

After supper Mary sat dazed on the sofa. Her guard was down. Oddly, Judith did not leap at this opportunity to pester. She ignored Mary. Mother and Papa listened to the radio. No one dared interrupt while Nellie McClung spoke soberly about the recent struggle to get women officially declared persons. Then Mother and Papa chuckled through the "Air Adventures of Jimmy Allen."

In the next fifteen-minute segment, the station broadcast "Heart-throbs of the Hills." Everyone was listening. Mary thought of Jessy lying under a hill of snow. They were both alone. She hated that radio, which pushed aside her troubles. Her heart throbbed with pain. Her love for Jessy was being frozen inside her. She saw the gray face sink away, smothered under a weight of snow, deep, airless, loveless. Each breath seemed harder to find.

Mary went up to bed and cried herself to sleep. The next day she went digging. Judith and Joseph helped, and they soon had the area around the north window completely trampled. Yet as Mary had feared, they found no sign of Jessy.

"You might have left her in the root cellar," Judith said.

"I doubt it." They checked anyway. Judith helped her down the ladder into the hole. Deep in the ground, a smell of potatoes and dirt and cabbage and squash pressed heavily on Mary. "See, she's not here either."

"Have you tried the hayloft?" Judith asked.

"No." Wearily, Mary climbed the ladder out of that deep pit in the earth, closed the door of the tiny shed, which was also its roof, and ran to the barn.

"We're gonna try the hayloft, Papa," Judith shouted.

He was hard at work, heaving manure over the chewed boards of the calf pen. It landed with a thud in the wheelbarrow. "You do that," he grunted.

They climbed up the ladder. The rungs were almost too far apart for Mary to manage. Up top, the air felt warmer and the hay smelled sweet. She looked feverishly for Jessy.

Judith flopped onto a low mound of hay. "I just can't think what could have become of your dolly," she said. "How would you like to play with Candy instead?"

"No, thanks."

Judith flapped her arms as if making a snow angel, then rolled off and stood up. She stared down at the shape she'd left in the straw. "My new invention," she said. "It's a hay angel."

Chapter 9

Mary didn't want to give up so easily. And she certainly didn't want to play with Judith's doll. With her smiling ceramic face, and pink hands and feet, Candy was cold and lifeless. She was a pretty doll, but a doll just the same. Jessy knew Mary's world, which Candy never could. When a doll was born in Papa's barn instead of bought in town at a stranger's store, everything was different.

But it was a generous offer, especially coming from Judith. "No, thank you very much, Judith," Mary said. She dug into a tall mound of hay, dug until she set a hay slide in motion. Dust particles flew up and drifted like clouds across the slats of sunlight squeezing between the barn boards. Mary kicked through the dusty hay and peeked into musty corners, determined to find her baby. How could she have let Jessy out of her sight for one minute?

She peered into a pigeon nest that straddled a large beam. Nothing.

At supper Papa asked, "So then, did you find your doll, Mary?"

"No, Papa," answered Judith. "And we looked everywhere."

Papa looked at Judith. Her face froze into that about-to-whine cast she always wore around him. "I appreciate the way you're taking an interest in this," he said.

Judith sat up and beamed. "We still have a few places to look, I think."

Papa wiped his mouth. "Well, thank you for the effort. Even if you don't find her, you've tried, and that's all we can ask, isn't it, Mother?"

"That's right," said Mother. "Judith, you've been wonderful through all of this."

"Well, I...I...," Judith said shakily, then shrugged.

"Go on," Papa said.

Judith looked up. "I'll take Mary's turn drying dishes tonight."

Papa raised his eyebrows. "Whoa! Above and beyond the call of duty! Do we have a new daughter on our hands?" His blue eyes studied Judith, who blushed back to her ears.

Mother put down her fork. "Raynold, she's just trying to help."

"Won't hear no complaints from me."

"Well, you don't have to scare her off."

"Yessiree!" Papa said, saluting briskly. He winked at Judith and then at Mary. They both wiggled on their hard wooden chairs and giggled at his impertinence toward Mother. It had been such a somber supper. Anything light, anything at all, was a welcome relief.

"What about me, Papa?" shouted Joseph. "What about me?"

"Oh! Sorry, son!" Papa gave Joseph a salute and a wink. Joseph winked back by blinking both eyes. Then he tried to salute and stuck his thumb into his right eye socket. His eye watered, his eyelid quivered and his lip came out. As everyone laughed at him, he took only a moment to decide not to cry. Then he poked himself again.

"Joseph, stop it," said Mother. "You'll put your eye out."

"Remember when I was a sheep in the Christmas play?" said Judith. "All the grade fours wanted to be animals, but me and Annie and Noelle won. Everyone else got the long straws. I was supposed to be a cow, but in practice Andy, the shepherd, tripped over me on the way to the manger, and I made a bleat like a sheep. Everyone laughed so hard that I became a sheep. Andy took off one of Theresa's angel wings too, when he fell over me, and then he knocked off Anthony's turban—he was the taller wise man—knocked

81

off his turban with that shepherd's crook of his, reckless boy."

In spite of her recent loss, Mary found herself caught up in Judith's story. Imagining herself as the entire cast at once, she felt the shepherd boy trip over her back, she sensed her angel wing fall away through the air, and she saw that long crook reach for her turban.

"Yes, you made an excellent sheep," said Papa. "I was all set to bring that sheep home to fatten for Mother's pot!"

Even Mother laughed at that one.

Mary thought about the wing and the turban flying. She saw the crook on the shepherd's staff swinging, she saw the boy lying in a tangle over the bleating sheep and she saw her sister untangling herself. Mary giggled on through the meal.

When supper came to an end, Mother said, "Well, Mary, it wasn't that funny!" But Mother was grinning in spite of herself.

"Let me tell you a story then," said Mary. "It's a story about Judith the sheep, about boys tripping over her and purple turbans." Her body convulsed with excitement. "Then angels were shrieking, 'Surprise! Hosanna Gloria!' Wise men were counting by night. They're old men hollering at each other because they're hitting each other with the crook, and Judith's a bleating sheep who butts them off the stage." She butted her head up and squealed at this mental picture. Judith and Joseph and Papa laughed along with her, but not Mother.

Mother's brow furrowed. Before Mary had a chance to end her story, Mother said, "Let's rein ourselves in, now, shall we? Come help me do these dishes. That'll steady you down. There's no point in letting yourself go berserk."

Mary looked at Judith. In everybody's hearing, Judith had offered to do the dishes for Mary. Judith stared at her empty plate. Then Mary realized how ridiculous that was. How foolish to expect favors from her sister.

Mary cleared the table. While she was drying the plates, Judith came from behind and took the dishtowel from her. "You go listen to the radio with Papa," she said. "I promised."

"Thank you!" Astonished, Mary skipped away to the living room, where the radio was hissing in the corner. A group of men began to sing "Sweet Adeline." Judith and Mother finished the dishes and sat down in time for a radio game of some kind, which Mary didn't understand and could barely hear in any case because of Papa's snoring.

Papa took up the entire sofa, and Mary half-listened from the floor beside him. Then she fell asleep. She woke up and Judith was lying on the floor beside her.

"Shh!" Papa said before anyone could utter a word.

"Farmers at the meeting maintained the native pasture is damaged so badly it will be some years before it will be of any use. Livestock cannot get anything to eat even in the seeded crops, and the government is planning more relief efforts. Local grain crops did not grow last year and are not expected to grow this year due to drifting dust and precipitation levels about half of normal. The price of grain has been trading higher lately, close to a dollar per bushel, but the drought has reduced production averages to eight bushels per acre from our 1928 high of twenty-three bushels. The farmers were very concerned about the twelve thousand Saskatchewan farms abandoned last year alone. The prospect for 1937 is grim indeed, and our weather office predicts severe dust storms will sweep the area once more this coming season."

Papa and Mother looked at each other with tears in their eyes.

Judith groaned. Mary went to bed.

In the morning, when Mary woke, bright bars of sunlight streamed through the shutters. Narrow bands of yellow light stepped across the quilt. She reached lazily to the pillow beside her. But Jessy was not there.

After feeling all about and under the pillow, Mary remembered. Jessy was no longer with them. All day yesterday they had searched and searched in vain. She was lost somewhere in the snow, perhaps worse. After too short a time together, she and Jessy had been parted.

Mary began to cry, quietly at first, but then she let the tears come. She was alone. Everything good had begun with Jessy, and now, so soon, it was ending. The hole in her heart felt like it must be getting bigger. Then a strange thing happened. A warm arm came from Judith's side of the bed, wrapped itself around Mary's shoulders and held her tightly.

Expecting a vicious pinch, Mary tensed. But there was no pain. If an arm could be friendly, this one certainly was. And Judith had done the dishes. Mary's panic eased off. The heat and pressure of that thin arm gave her some comfort. The slender fingers that had once twisted any bit of bare skin, stroked Mary's hair.

Maybe, mused Mary, she was not quite alone. With all these people around, there was no need to be alone. But she had to wonder why Judith had waited so long to be friendly. It felt nice, but Mary didn't say anything. At this point the wrong words might ruin everything.

Chapter 10

Judith approached Mary with an envelope. "Here," she said. "We made them in school. Next year you will too."

What a strange feeling it was to accept something from Judith. Less than a week had passed, and she and Judith were inseparable. From the moment of that encircling arm, the two girls had eaten together, played together after school and helped each other with chores. Late at night they talked. As moonbeams inched across their bed, they told each other about when they would marry and planned how they would live in Davidson across the street from each other. They would visit each other and send their children to visit each other too. For Christmas and Easter they would send their husbands to the farm to pick up Mother and Joseph and Papa, if he'd come, and they'd all go to church. Their husbands would drive shiny new cars, not old jalopies pulled by horses.

Mary didn't really plan to give up the farm and her valley so easily, nor Papa and Mother, nor Clyde, but she did want to play along with Judith. The past days had been full of stunning moments, and now Judith was giving her something that she had made.

"What is it?" Mary asked.

"For Valentine's Day."

"What's that?"

"Open it and see."

A small card was tucked into the envelope. A big heart, colored red with crayon, had been drawn on the card-face, and a horseshoe of words was placed unevenly around this heart. "What are these words?" Judith's printing wasn't the best.

Judith pointed at each word. "Won't you be my Valentine? Love, Judith."

"Won't you be my Valentine? Wow!"

"Yes, wow!"

"But Judith, what does it mean?"

"It means I'm happy to be your sister, and I hope we'll be friends forever. I made one for Papa too, and Mother."

The news that others were also to receive valentines made Mary's seem a little less special, but all in all she was happy to get anything nice from Judith. She sure didn't want to go back to being enemies. And she couldn't afford to lose any friends.

"Miss Catherine says the winter storms are all but through," Judith said, sipping her make-believe tea. They were celebrating the Ides of March by having a tea party up in the hayloft.

"Yes, darling," said Mary, mimicking the voice of Calphurnia, wife of Julius Caesar in the play on the radio the night before. "I do believe winter has passed off rather marvellously this year. Is your Miss Catherine well?"

"Rumor has it she has found a new beau."

"What's a beau?"

"A boyfriend, like mine."

"You have a boyfriend? You don't say!"

"Yes, Andy Spearman."

"Who's he?"

"You must remember, my precious, that fine dear boy who tripped over me at Christmas. But keep it secret or I'll simply die."

"Awww! Even from Papa?"

"Especially from Papa."

Mary didn't know if she'd be able to manage that, but Judith looked at her so intently she had to agree. "Okay, I promise." Sipping her tea, Mary thought she'd never be able to wait to go to school and have a boyfriend. She sighed and looked back at Judith. Who could have guessed that this sister, only one year older, lived such a secret and glamorous life?

Judith stopped at the pump to wash off the potatoes and carrots. They were growing long white roots, but still usable. Mary climbed up out of the cool root cellar as loud hammering noises began nearby. They seemed to come from behind the barn. She closed the door.

"Is that Papa or Joseph?"

"Let's go find out what's happening back there," Judith answered.

They found Papa working on the buggy. The buggy was parked between the plow and the truck, both idle now. To plow, Papa had to borrow two extra horses. To operate the truck, he had to find money for an expensive part.

Waiting for him to become aware of them, Judith cleared her throat politely. Mary coughed. They giggled.

"So, the days are getting longer, girls," Papa said finally. He lifted his eyes to them but left his fingers clamped around the buggy springs.

"I hardly noticed," Judith replied.

This surprised Mary. "What about Miss Catherine?" she asked.

"What about her?"

Taking up a brush, Papa applied grease to the buggy axle.

"About her saying winter is all but through?"

Judith shrugged.

Mary shrugged too. But how could Judith not notice

spring? The sun went higher with each pass. She and Joseph were shedding clothes like wolves shed fur. Spring was most notable by the Arm, whose ice had cracked and been swept downstream. The willows were in leaf. Papa said all this was due to some early rain and a whole lot of heat. The frog opera, as he called it, had opened two nights before. All along the river, froggy voices lifted to the evening sky, singing like choirs of angels. Antelope raced up the empty valley, tearing at the first grass, then running off in search of whatever antelopes searched for. Away from the river, green shoots found a way through the yellow mat of last year's grass and weeds. Ducks and geese glided overhead or splashed into shrinking puddles on the bare fields. How could you not notice leaving winter coats indoors? Mary guessed Judith must be pulling her leg, since they agreed on practically every topic these days.

Papa stood and looked at his work. "Well, live and learn, daughter. When Mother gets to fussing about Easter, watch for the days to get longer."

"Mother says today is Good Friday," said Judith. "Why does she call it good if someone got murdered?"

"Good question. You better ask her. She's the expert." Papa dropped his brush into the grease can. He rolled the big spindly wheel into position and slid its hub onto the axle. He threaded on a nut. "Soon you'll be home all the time, not just during storms, or holidays like today."

Papa hadn't glanced at Judith, but she smiled. "I don't mind. Mary and I will carry water to the garden this summer and go to school together in the fall."

How far their friendship had come! It was one thing for Judith not to mind staying home on a holiday, quite another for her to plan her whole summer around working together.

"Everyone helping out as they can. That's our best chance for surviving this year," said Papa. "Mother and I are talking seed. It's the same old dream about this time every year. Probably turn to grief on us too." He sighed, looked at his daughters and smiled. "Escape from that winter-bound house don't seem to matter as much this spring. I have to say, Judith, that you've been a pleasure to us all."

Judith blushed deeply.

Mary laughed. Her heart felt light as a spring breeze.

Chapter 11

Two days later, Mary woke early. Excitement gripped her. They were all to go to town. It was so early that no sunrays had yet pierced her windowpane, but the sparrows had begun to argue in the lilac bush beneath the window. She slipped out of her warm bed, trying not to chafe the cotton and so wake Judith. Mary swooped her clothes off the floor, tiptoed past the sleeping Joseph and pulled on her clothes in the dark stairway.

Her jacket and boots on, she went outside into the crisp air of a prairie morning. The air shimmered with spring, right up to the last few stars, which welcomed Mary with open arms. She stood on the porch step, listening to an exchange between the rooster, whose muffled challenge came from inside the barn, and a crow. The crow rasped first from the peak of the root-cellar shed, and a short flight later from the handle of the water pump. Its feathers gleamed a beautiful blue-black against a dull land-scape that was still mostly brown.

"Easter," Mary breathed. Today she would go to the schoolhouse again, or at least close to it. Did Judith know where they would both sit in the fall? Mary would try for Papa's old desk. She could hardly wait for the trip into town. She jumped off the step, not knowing what to do first. Papa was in the barn, jetting milk out of Laura. Mary heard that familiar pattering *preesh*, *preesh*, *preesh* against the bottom of his pail. The milk was about to deepen and go *shwoosh*, *shwoosh*, *shwoosh* and produce a fine froth. He had barely started chores, then. Mary thought it best to leave him alone.

The sun peeked over the horizon, painting the entire farm with a reddish hue. Mary walked around the little shed that was the entrance to the root cellar. Its boards were a bright gray, grainy, wet with dew. A pair of ducks sped by overhead, quacking happily at the prospect of another day dunking for tidbits in the sloughs, or drifting on the Arm. Clyde was in his corral, eating a hay breakfast and snorting with contentment. Moving to the west side of the house, Mary saw Mother. Delighted at being able to share such a morning, she ran over.

Mother stood on the gentle rise between the outhouse and the prairie-dog town. Her head was hanging low. A basket full of brightly colored eggs dangled from her hand.

Mary knew which eggs she had painted herself and which were the work of Judith or Joseph.

"What are you doing, Mother?"

"Just seeing after my little angel." Mother nodded downward to indicate a cross stuck in the ground.

The cross, painted white only months ago, was streaked with grime. It was a marker for a small low mound of naked dirt. A few feet away, a second cross, now aged, stood at the head of a second mound, one covered in the yellow-brown grass that ran off wild and flat in every direction, except for the few brown squares of Papa's fields between the barn and the Arm. Mary inhaled the scent of damp dried grass. "Is the little angel still here?" she asked, suddenly confused. Angels were supposed to fly up in the yellow air.

"Not really. She lives out there." Mother lifted her arm toward the eastern sky, which they faced. The sky was alive with fire, a cool red burning. The sun grew huge, expanding upward. Like a ball on the horizon, it looked ready to bounce into the red air. After a minute, Mother added, "But we put the cross here."

"Why? What do you mean?"

Mother stared at the brown mound of dirt. "Hmm?"

"The little angel," Mary prompted, feeling a pang of worry at this strange behavior. Was the trip to town about to be cancelled?

"Yes, dear. Sometimes she and I meet here at the grave."

"To talk?"

"Something like that." Mother glanced at Mary with a reassuring smile.

Then Mary felt a hand wiggle into her own. Judith had joined them. Mary squeezed gently. Judith grabbed Mother's hand too. Their faces were lovely in the light. But the rest of Judith looked a sight! Her barn coat, which did not smell at all fresh, had been thrown on hastily. The front was buttoned askew. Her nightgown stuck out below the coat, clinging to two white legs that were bare down into her muddy boots.

"What's the rush?" asked Mary. "Afraid of missing out on the fun?"

Judith's face looked beautiful, but worried. "Let's go back and wake up Joseph, and then we can do the eggs." She glanced past the graves and pulled at Mary's hand.

The early morning rays washed Judith and Mother to a lively wonderful pink.

The reddish light struck the ground around them, then skidded upward. Just beyond the little mound and its little cross, about where Judith had glanced, the light shone on a tuft of new grass. It grew in Papa's special little flower garden, bare and dark brown for the moment, with its neat wall of stones to protect his flowers from the bitter north winds. Now that's odd, thought Mary. Grass growing in that one spot of dirt and nowhere else? How could that grass be such a bright green and everything she stood on be so yellow? "Look at the funny grass," she said, pointing with her free hand. Pulling her other hand free of Judith's grip, she walked over to look more closely. The grass grew roughly in the shape of a star.

No, the grass grew exactly in the shape of a star.

"Look," she said, laughing, "this grass is growing just like Jessy. Here's the head and body, and these are the arms and legs. See how the little arms stop just before the hands." Mary swung her eyes over to see if Judith was laughing at the funny way this grass grew.

But Judith was not laughing. Her face cringed. A stranger had taken over Judith's fine features. And in this light her sister seemed treacherous again, ready to pinch.

Mary looked at the bright grass, then at Mother. With a sudden certainty that made her legs quake, Mary understood. "It is Jessy!"

Chapter 12

"Mother," she cried, "Judith buried Jessy here!" Anger flared in Mary's throat and spread into her stomach. Her hands shook.

Mother leaned down to examine Judith, who looked up tearfully. A tear formed in the corner of Mother's eye too, and she released Judith's hand to wipe it away.

"It is Jessy," Judith admitted. With a terrified look, she grabbed at Mother's hand.

"Why?"

Judith shrugged, put her hands into her coat pockets and stared at the mud on her boots. "I buried her at the end of that chinook, when we had to close the shutters."

"But why?" Mother repeated.

"You of all people should know why."

"Tell me anyway."

"Why does Mary get everything?"

"That was a nasty thing to do."

"I had to. Papa never even saw me." Judith sounded miserable.

"That's plain mean, Judith. Don't blame Papa for your own shortcomings."

Mary remembered that morning long before when Papa's new radio was set up in the kitchen. Papa had said the day that Jessy woke up and helped with chores would be the day their troubles would end. That same day, a big storm of hail had come and drummed on the barn. And she'd searched the entire farm for Jessy, who had been pushed down into the mud.

"You got shoes for Christmas, the one thing your sister wanted, and you had to hide her homemade gift, the only thing she got."

Judith's eyes were glued to the ground. Huge tears rolled down her pink cheeks. "No, Mother, she had everything. She had Papa and she had you."

"Had me? No more than you!"

"Yes, and Papa too. You know it's true."

Mother looked at the ground speechlessly.

As the shock of the morning's discovery flowed through her, Mary stood stock-still. She wasn't going to be able to forgive Judith for stealing Jessy. That was certain. That was too much to ask. Judith got the shoes, and she got the nosebag. Judith buried Jessy.

As if she couldn't tolerate Mary's eyes on her another moment, Judith put her face against Mother's waist and began to sob.

Mary's fingers tingled with rage. She saw Jessy's face pressed down into the mud, saw the old canvas tear under Judith's heel, saw the oat seeds leak out and sprout in the too early heat. Would this Depression never end? She was willing to bet she still had that hole in her heart, too, and wouldn't be allowed to attend school.

Shaking herself, Mary looked around. They all stood on this spreading yellow grass under this huge living sky. Her mother and her sister and herself all seemed so small.

Mary didn't know what to do, but suddenly, studying that sky, she did feel sure that Judith was sorry for what she had done. Mary remembered how bad she had felt after losing Jessy, and how Judith had held her and how they became instant friends. Now Judith had confessed.

"What do I say, Mother?" Mary asked.

Mother shook her head.

"I'm sorry," said Judith, wiping her face on her sleeve and pushing away from Mother. "I was mean to do that. I'll do anything to make it up."

There didn't seem to be anything to do, though. And how could Judith undo burying Jessy? There seemed to be no way back. "I'm sorry too," Mary said.

"You're sorry?" Judith asked anxiously.

"Yes. I was mean too." She only said this to give herself time to think, but now that the words were out, Mary knew they were true. She'd been mean to Judith. So often she had been glad that Judith wasn't Papa's girl, like she was.

Judith allowed herself a small nod and a smile.

"But that's over with, right?"

Judith, red-eyed, nodded.

"I'm sorry too," Mother said. She stroked Judith's head.

The barn door slammed. Mary ran back past the house to get Papa. She returned in minutes with him in tow. Judith and Mother were hugging each other. When she pulled Papa past the little mounds with their small crosses, Mary pointed at the star of short green grass and said, "Look, Papa, we found Jessy."

"Sure, sweetheart," he said, patting her head.

Mary stamped her foot. "No! It is her growing here, Papa! See? Head, arms, legs, just like you made her." With both hands she followed the outline of the blunt green star on the ground. "See? Our troubles are over, like you said."

"I never said our troubles were over!"

"Jessy helped with chores, like you said. She started seeding the new crop."

"Oh, that," said Mother, with an intake of breath, nodding. "I remember."

"Can someone let me in on this?"

Papa looked at Mother. Raising her eyebrows, she said, "The two of them are friends now, Ray. You can hardly deny that." Bent over Judith, she rocked them both back and forth. Their bodies made a red knot in the red light.

Judith looked sideways at Mary and tried a smile.

Mary beamed back at her. Were all their troubles over? Not really. But some were. At the least, she and Judith would go to school together as friends.

"You're not angry?" Judith asked. She pushed away from Mother again, delicate as an antelope ready to spring away up the valley.

Mary almost said, "Yes," but then shook her head. She'd never give up Judith now, not for the world. Judith's face relaxed into a beautiful pinkness, a perfect flower under a sky that had never looked quite so clear. "Look, Papa," said Mary, "it's a real blue sky finally too."

"Angry at what?" Papa asked, glancing at each of them in turn.

Mother held out one of her hands. "Come here," she said. She leaned down to hug Mary and squeezed Judith with her other arm. "You two are so precious to me." Letting them go, Mother straightened up. She was taller than Mary remembered. One of her fine hands reached down for the handle of her basket.

"What does a bit of grass prove?" Papa asked.

"Come on," said Mother. "Let's get ready for church."

They moved toward the house. It was a dark block in the light. Its roof wedged up into the sky. On the peak of the roof balanced the risen sun. It seemed ready to fall off to either side, thought Mary, but that sun was burning with the strength of spring. It wouldn't fall off. She wanted to go to town, to school, to sing in church.

She wanted to run, anywhere, everywhere.

The long shadow of the house lay on the ground. They stood at its edge. Mary ran off the shadow, wondering if light could ever make noise. If it could, this sunrise would be swishing and frothing around them like new milk. The valley was a wide bowl that contained all it could, right up to the brim of its graceful sides. Just then a pair of snow geese glided by overhead, their white feathers gathering the valley's glow. Mary could hear their wings slice through the soft spring air. Honking, the birds turned and flapped away over the Arm. Joining hands and flying over the red-tinted ground, Mary and Judith skipped circles around their parents.

Mother and Papa were walking away slowly, talking quietly. A gentle breeze pushed Mother's dress so it fluttered away from her legs. It was another warm morning.

"Wait," said Judith. "Let's stash the eggs. Then Joseph can hunt them down."

They ran into the shadow where their parents walked and chose two eggs.

Judith clamped her eyelids shut. "You go first," she said.

Mary didn't know where to hide her egg. It was a beauty, sky blue, one of Judith's best. Only a really good spot could do it justice. A prairie dog squeaked from the burrows, inviting Mary out toward the brown mounds of dog town. She ran out to the two little angels' mounds. Where should I hide this egg? Mary wondered. Looking down, she knew. She placed the egg gently on Jessy's green face. It was an eye of blue to help her see the sky. The sky arced lovely and clean above them.

Clamping her hands over her eyes, smiling with joy, Mary called out, "Your turn!"

A minute or so went by. "Done!"

Mary dropped her hands. Now her parents were sitting on the back step of the house, holding the basket between them. They were looking up at the blue sky. Running home to them, Mary and Judith each picked up two more eggs.

"Hurry now," said Mother. "I can hear your brother waking up already. And it's time to get the tea going."

Breathless, the girls nodded and ran off again.

"Mary! Got your eyes closed?"

"Bet your muddy boots I do!"

The basket emptied slowly. Mary ran faster, hiding eggs in clever places like mouse tunnels in the grass or on top of fence posts. Judith was busy out at the prairie-dog town. After she had set an egg in an empty flower tub, Mary watched Mother and Papa jump up, grab a handful of brightly colored eggs each and run away to hide them.

Only two eggs were left, a fine green one Judith had painted and a milky blue one of Mary's. Mary reached for them just as Joseph pushed his uncombed head out the back door. Grinning into his sleepy face, she hid them behind her and backed away. At the corral, where Clyde munched placidly on his breakfast as if nothing ever happened, she set her eggs in the dead weeds by the water trough. Ears forward, Clyde sniffed them and shook his head. The eggs did not smell like hay or sugar or carrots or apples or grass, or like the oats he so loved.

Mary squinted up into his long mild face and stroked a finger across his velvet lip. Smiling, she returned to the house. Her sister and mother and father sat waiting for her on the sun-washed front steps. Soon they'd hitch up the buggy and go to town.

Her brother ran around the corner of the house. He was shaking the empty egg basket. "I wanted to hide them too!" he said, beginning to pout.

"There's none left to hide," Judith said. Her arms spread out to embrace the valley.

"True," said Mary, giggling up at the bright blue sky, "but there's lots left to find. And every last one of them is stashed in a very good spot."

Acknowledgements

In the early 1990s, my father-in-law, John Doerksen, who had been a prairie farm boy himself during the Great Depression of the 1930s, told me the kernel of this story. I thought about that little oat-filled doll all summer. What family situation would produce the chain of events he described? What would make a child bury her sister's doll? I pried for more details. John claimed it had happened to people a few farms over from where he lived. He had no other details to give. Finally I sat down and wrote out my own explanation. I believe he was proud of my attempt, although he did not survive to read the book.

I can't (really, I can't) let this book go to press without thanking my wife, Karen, who read less-readable versions but always believed. Likewise, my friend Fred Meissner read and commented on the text with a poet's heart. In this group I must include Maggie de Vries at Orca Book Publishers, whose iron will and light touch graces each page.

I'd also like to thank Heather Marshall and Debbie Culbertson and Professor Keith Harder for believing in this book and doing everything they could to help get it to the public. Thank you to Neil Hultin for those juicy bits of historical detail. Thanks in particular to my snap-happy sister, Theresa, for the photo shoot in Calgary, and thanks generally both to Karen's family and my own family for their interest over the years.

Finally, I haven't forgotten the friends who have read or listened to the story and have been moved, as I have, by Mary and Judith and a homemade doll with no nose or hair.

And thank you too, Reader, whether your nose be satisfactory, whether your hair is coming in or falling out. May you be moved as well.

photo credit: Theresa Simons

Joseph Simons was an avid reader as a child and remains one to this day. He is intimately acquainted with farm life, right down to the calluses on his hands. He loves Saskatchewan, where he lived in the early 1980s, except for the winters, which, he says, "Demand another kind of thinking about one's place in the world." Still, even in those winters, Joseph rode his bike to work every day. He based *Under a Living Sky* on a story that his late father-in-law told him, a story that he could not shake. *Under a Living Sky* is his first book. Visit him at www.josephsimons.ca.